THE BRIDAL SHOWER

A PSYCHOLOGICAL SUSPENSE THRILLER

N. L. HINKENS

Text copyright @ 2025 Norma Hinkens

Published by Dunecadia Publishing, California

ISBN: 978-1-947890-54-1

Cover by: https://www.derangeddoctordesign.com/

Editing by: https://www.jeanette-morris.com/first-impressions-writing/

DEDICATION

For Charity, the best mother-in-law my daughter could ever have asked for.

1

"Happy birth-day, dear Lau-ra," I sing at the top of my lungs, a plastic smile printed on my lips.

My future mother-in-law beams around the table at everyone, soaking up her moment in the sun.

Truthfully, I'm having doubts about marrying Chad. He's not the problem per se—it's the marrying-into-his-family part that's giving me gut-wrenching nightmares. The closer we get to the wedding, the more desperate my mother-in-law becomes. She acts as though I'm stealing her son with some malevolent purpose in mind. She became pregnant with Chad after a decade of infertility, which might explain in part why she's so possessive of him. I'm not sure why she despises me so much, but she never wastes an opportunity to remind me how much she adored Chad's first wife, Shana. It's hard competing with a dead woman who's been elevated to sainthood.

"Thank you, everyone," Laura gushes. "Now, let's cut that delicious-looking cake." She leans over and pats me on the knee. "You really can't hold a note, dear. You should consider toning it down a bit."

Beneath the table I curl my hands into fists, trying to extinguish the longing to box her into oblivion. I'm only letting the insult slide because Chad asked me to overlook any barbs she fires my way today.

"It's hard not to be exuberant," I say, serving up my reply with an edge of tartness. "It is your birthday, after all."

Laura gives a wistful nod, cocking her head to one side. " Shana always played 'Happy Birthday' on the piano for me. Chad's wife was such a gifted pianist. I miss her terribly on these kinds of occasions."

Chad's wife. Does she have to remind me that Shana came first every time she mentions her? I reach for the serrated knife on the table and slash it through the cake.

"Who's having a slice?" I call out, grinning as though I haven't a care in the world. Inwardly I'm fighting the murderous call of my heart. I wish I could simply say that my mother-in-law infuriates me, but the truth is, she brings out something buried in the dark recesses of my innards that terrifies me.

Martina, my best friend and maid of honor, cautioned me months ago against marrying Chad.

"His mother's only fifty-two," she pointed out over drinks one night after work. "Are you willing to endure that nagging, nitpicking cow for another thirty or forty years?"

I shrugged as I fished the cherry out of my spicy rum margarita. "I love her son."

"Chad's not the only decent guy out there, Eva. That witch is going to be in your business every minute of every day, and not for the right reasons. Can you seriously picture her as the grandmother of your kids?"

I shuddered at the thought and took a hasty gulp of my cocktail. "We can always move out of state."

"She'll follow you," Martina warned me. "Women like

that are relentless. She'll buy the house next door and haunt you for the rest of your days with unsolicited advice. If you ask me, you should run while you still have the chance."

I shake myself free of the memory as I slice up the cake and pass the plates around the table, beginning with her majesty, Laura. It's times like this I'm tempted to throw in the towel and walk away from a future with Chad. I wish my parents were still alive so there was someone in my court to advise me. They were killed in a car crash five years ago and I miss them more every day. Chad's father died of a heart attack when he was in high school—I can't help thinking it had something to do with the stress of being married to Laura.

She peers at the piece of cake on her plate, frowning. " Oh my, that's quite the hack job, isn't it? Don't worry, dear. I know you're trying."

I grit my teeth, forcing myself to concentrate on finishing the task at hand instead of responding the way I'd like by stuffing the entire slice into her mouth and slamming her jaw shut so she chokes on it. I glance over at Chad who's busy brewing a pot of coffee. He gives me a sympathetic smile, his brown eyes pooling with gratitude for my endurance of another marathon session of passive-aggressive tongue lashing. We've had more than one conversation about how much I'm willing to put up with going forward. I've made it clear to Chad that, after we're married, I need to be his top priority.

"I think Mom's having a hard time accepting you because it means accepting that Shana is gone," Chad explained to me after one particularly heated discussion. "They were very close."

"No kidding," I huffed. "She never stops going on about Shana this, and Shana that."

Chad simply rubbed a hand over his jaw, looking uncomfortable. I don't blame him. What's he supposed to say to a fiancée who's jealous of his dead wife? Not to mention the fact that his own mother is constantly stoking the flames. That's above most men's pay grade.

"Time to open presents," Laura chirps, clapping her hands like an overgrown child.

Brandy, her daughter, picks up a gift bag and passes it to her. "This is from me, Mom."

"Thank you, honey!" Laura plucks out several sheets of pink tissue paper and peers into the bag. "My favorite perfume! How did you know I was out?"

Brandy chuckles as she catches my eye. "Well, you did mention it once or twice."

Laura gives herself a couple of squirts on each wrist, and I wrinkle my nose, trying not to show my disgust at the overpowering musky stench that wafts my way.

"This one's from me," I say, handing her a small, gift-wrapped box. "Happy Birthday."

Laura picks unsuccessfully at the tape with her acrylic nails. "Fetch me some scissors, would you, Eva? I must say I do prefer a gift bag to wrapping paper. I find it so wasteful throwing it away afterward."

I hand her the scissors, trying, unsuccessfully, not to picture them sticking out the side of her throat. "Here you go."

She slices open the tape and lifts the lid of the box inside, revealing the necklace I spent a fair chunk of change on, not to mention hours agonizing over.

"Oh, how ... whimsical." She dangles it on the end of her finger for everyone to see before dropping it back in the box. Turning to me, she mutters, "Did you keep the receipt, dear?"

I flash her a bright smile. "Of course not. I knew you'd love it."

She stiffens, her eyes narrowing to thin slits. I can almost hear her hissing at me. One thing is clear. There isn't room for both of us in Chad's life. If marrying him means I have to listen to my future mother-in-law ranting about my long litany of inadequacies and flaws for the rest of my life, I might just have to kill her.

2

—————

"Don't forget I have my dress fitting after work today, and I'm going out with the girls afterward," I say to Chad on the phone. I reach for my coat as I head out the door of the apartment I share with my older sister, Robin.

"No worries," he replies. "I'm going to the gym with a couple of guys from work."

I fumble around in my purse for my keys. "I gotta go. I'm already running a few minutes late and this week's going to be crazy busy with trial prep."

"Wait! I wanted to ask you something."

"What?" I ask, trying to curb my impatience.

"I know this is a big ask," Chad begins in a cajoling tone, "but Mom's really upset you didn't ask her to go dress shopping. Any chance you could invite her along to the fitting?"

I toss my head in frustration. "I didn't invite her because she would have hated everything I put on. I don't want her spoiling every memory associated with my wedding. It was a perfect day without her."

Chad lets out a weighty sigh. "I'm glad it was perfect. But this is just a fitting. You've already picked out your dress. Mom can't influence your choice now."

"Fine," I say shrugging on my coat. "But if she breathes one word to you about my dress, I'm uninviting her to the wedding. So, you'd better warn her."

Chad chuckles. "Nothing will induce her to miss the wedding. I'm sure she'll be on her best behavior."

I roll my eyes. "Which isn't saying much."

I EXIT the law office where I work as a legal intern shortly after 5:00 p.m. and make the ten-minute walk to the bridal store where I purchased my dress. Robin waves to me as she exits her car and hurries to meet me.

"Are you excited to try on your dress?" she asks.

I grimace. "Laura's going to be putting in an appearance, so that's put a damper on things."

Robin's brows shoot up. "What possessed you to invite her?"

I shrug. "Chad talked me into it. She's still whining to him about the fact that I didn't invite her to go dress shopping. And she's been mouthing off about me to neighbors, and relatives, and anyone who will listen for weeks on end, telling them I'm being mean, and isolating her from her son. She even posted derogatory things about me on social media. I'd like nothing more than to ring her neck, but I'm trying to keep the peace—at least until the wedding's over."

Robin pulls the door to the bridal shop open and we walk into the reception where Martina is lounging on a tufted couch.

She squeals when she sees me and jumps up to hug me.

"I'm bursting with excitement. Aren't you just dying to see what your dress looks like on?"

Her smile falters when she sees the expression on my face.

"There's been a slight hiccup," Robin informs her. "The cantankerous cow is joining us."

Martina's eyes widen in horror. "No! Tell me you're joking."

"Ladies, this way please," the bridal assistant chirps as she glides into the room oblivious to the air of gloom that's descended on our party. She leads us to a private fitting room and hangs my dress on a hook inside the changing area. Martina and Robin take their seats on a velvet chaise, heads huddled together, no doubt discussing my mother-in-law's last minute intrusion on our plans. Thankfully, there's no sign of her yet. Fingers crossed, something's come up and she can't make it after all.

The bridal assistant holds my dress open for me so I can step into it. She carefully pulls it up and fastens the satin buttons on the back. All my frustration melts away when I look in the mirror and see how perfectly the sheath silhouette fits through the bodice and waist, effortlessly skimming my curves and falling straight down to the floor. "I love it," I say, a huge grin spreading over my face. The assistant opens the curtain, and I shuffle out and step up onto the riser.

"I'm going to cry," Robin says, flapping her fingers dramatically in front of her face.

"You look absolutely stunning!" Martina adds. "It's perfect."

"*There* you are!" Laura calls out, bustling around the corner. "You gave me the wrong address. How careless of you!" She sinks down in a chair and presses a hand to her chest. "I'm winded after that long walk."

"You must have misread my message," I say firmly. *Deliberately misread it, no doubt.*

"This is Laura, my future mother-in-law," I explain to the disconcerted assistant.

"Too bad you got the address mixed up," I go on in an overly cheery tone. "But you're here now and that's all that matters."

"Is ... this the dress?" Laura asks, running her eyes up and down me in a crestfallen manner.

I turn this way and that admiring my profile in the mirror, not bothering to reply. *What else would it be? She knows it's a fitting.*

The assistant fusses with my train and spreads it out for me to see the full effect.

"Doesn't she look fabulous?" Robin says.

"It's a ... pretty dress." Laura sniffs. "For the right person."

Robin arches a reproving brow. "Good thing the right person is wearing it then, isn't it?"

Laura drops her gaze and rummages around in her purse. She pulls out a tissue and makes a point of blowing her nose loudly. "Could someone fetch me a bottle of water? I'm feeling rather faint."

"Of course, I'll be right back," the bridal shop assistant replies, looking irked at the interruption. I imagine she's dealt with her fair share of attention-seeking mothers-in-law before, but Laura's certainly up there with the best of them.

The assistant returns a moment later with the water, then helps me back inside the changing room.

From behind the curtain I overhear Laura say, "Look at this, girls! This is my daughter-in-law, Shana, in her wedding dress. Wasn't she breathtaking?"

I grit my teeth, trying to restrain myself from stomping my mother-in-law's phone into the ground as I rip the curtain open. I'm not going to play second fiddle to Chad's first wife any longer. Laura needs to be taught a lesson.

3

I've been distracted at work all day trying to figure out how to go about laying down the law with Laura after the fiasco at the bridal boutique. She's not going to be a part of our lives after we get married, not unless she drastically changes her ways. Maybe I should stop beating around the bush and have an honest conversation with her about setting behavioral boundaries—basic expectations of common decency. I can cite plenty of examples of her rudeness and passive aggressive behavior, but she might not accept what I'm telling her.

I call Chad that afternoon and let him know that I'm going to invite his mother out for dinner, if she accepts.

"Seriously?" he says. "Wow, thanks, baby. I appreciate the effort you're making. If there's a way to find some common ground, I know you'll make it happen."

"I'll let you know how it goes," I promise him.

When I hang up, I dial Laura's number. It rings and rings and goes straight to voicemail. I shake my head in amusement. Her phone is never more than an inch from her fingertips. She's screening her calls and deliberately ignoring me. No doubt, she'll listen to the voicemail the minute I finish recording.

"Hey Laura, I'd like to take you out for a mother-and-daughter-in-law pre-wedding dinner tonight, if you're available."

Twenty minutes go by before she calls me back. "Well, this is a surprise, coming from you of all people," she says, tinkling a mocking laugh. "What's the purpose of this dinner? I'm not naïve enough to think there isn't something you intend to gain from it."

I chew on my lip, trying to whip my words into some kind of believable response. "I think it's important that the two main women in Chad's life come to some kind of agreement on boundaries, and how we're going to interact with one another going forward. After all, we both want what's best for him, and the last thing we want to do is make life more difficult for him by making him choose between us."

"Indeed!" Laura replies. "It's encouraging to hear that you're finally seeing sense. Why don't you make a reservation at The Chophouse. I've been hankering for a steak."

I grimace as I hang up. The Chophouse is the most expensive restaurant in town. The last time I checked, the steaks start at eighty dollars and every side is extra. Still, it's a small price to pay for peace if I can achieve it over a couple of glasses of red wine and an overpriced meal.

I manage to snag a reservation for 7:00 p.m. and make sure to arrive a few minutes early so Laura has nothing to complain about on that front. She glides into the restaurant right on the dot of seven, her crimson lips pressed into a tight slash as she greets me with a cursory nod. She hangs her purse on the back of her chair and seats herself without a word of greeting. Instead, she reaches for the menu and peruses it at length.

I rub my brow, determined not to start the night off on the wrong foot. "What's your favorite thing to eat here. Laura?"

She throws me a sharp look. "Why? Are you having trouble deciding? It's important to be confident in your decisions, Eva. Indecisive women make for worthless wives." She snaps the menu shut. "I'll have the New York strip steak."

"Grilled sea bass for me," I reply, silently fuming at her crass dig.

The waiter stops by to take our order and comes back with a bottle of red wine that Laura ordered, and that I've never heard of—likely the most expensive thing on the menu.

"Laura," I begin. "The reason I invited you to dinner tonight is because I wanted to discuss the dynamics of our relationship. I shouldn't have lost my temper like I did yesterday, and I apologize for yelling at you in the bridal store. Obviously, we both love Chad very much, but we haven't exactly gelled to this point as mother and daughter-in-law."

Laura blinks innocently at me over the rim of her wine glass. "It certainly hasn't been for lack of trying on my part. But I must say, dear, Shana was a lot easier to love. And you have to admit, you did look rather bulky in that dress."

My jaw drops. I'm not sure if the wine has loosened her tongue, or if this is just the beginning of the end for us, but this conversation is not going in the right direction, and my patience is wearing thin. Despite my best attempt to remain neutral, I can't help but feel hurt. Why am I even bothering to try with this woman who's so unashamedly obnoxious?

I take a sip of wine and steel myself, determined not to give up just yet. "Let's just get one thing straight. Shana is dead and I'm marrying your son, whether you like it or not."

A look of sheer terror races across her face. It's gone so quickly, I almost think I imagined it, except for the fact that her glass is shaking in her fingers.

4

I reach for the stack of mail inside my mailbox and take it into the apartment. I can hardly believe the bridal shower is tomorrow. Martina and Robin have rented a beautiful country house for the occasion. The setting is gorgeous—sprawling lawns, fountains, and eucalyptus trees—and I know I'll feel like a queen sitting there eating afternoon tea and opening gifts with friends and family. *And future family*. My stomach churns at the thought of my mother-in-law wagging her caustic tongue throughout. I haven't seen her since the disastrous dress fitting and dinner afterward, but I'm sure she's been badmouthing me to anyone who'll listen. She's growing more desperate to get rid of me the closer we get to the wedding. The feeling is mutual.

Admittedly, I lost it after she showed Martina and Robin the picture of Shana in her wedding dress. I had to call the bridal boutique afterward and apologize for my behavior. I was a screaming bridezilla. Laura left in tears—induced to garner sympathy, no doubt. She refused to concede that what she did was inappropriate. Martina and Robin took my side, of course, but I think even they were shocked at my explosive temper. It's something I've always struggled with, and Laura knows just how to trigger it. I'm determined to keep it in check at the bridal shower, no matter what comes out of Laura's wrinkled lips.

I toss the mail in a pile on the kitchen counter and set about boiling a pot of water for pasta. I've just finished making an Alfredo sauce when Robin walks in, still dressed in her scrubs.

"How was your day?" I ask.

"Busy. I did nine cleanings. Someone actually asked me if we sterilize our instruments between patients." She gives an amused shake of her head. "Considering how many hundreds of different bacterial species live in the mouth, it's the least we can do for paying customers." She sighs as she flops down in a chair. "Educating the public is arduous."

"At least it's the weekend. You're off duty placating patients until Monday."

"Yes! And your bridal shower is tomorrow." Robin rubs her hands together. "I can't wait to see what you get."

I dish up two generous bowls of pasta and carry them over to the table. "Fancy a glass of wine to celebrate?"

"Sure," Robin replies, inhaling the aroma of the pasta. "Mmm. This smells good."

I pour us each a glass, then take a seat at the table. "The only thing I'm worried about," I say between mouthfuls, "is coming face-to-face with Laura again. I haven't set eyes on her since the dress fitting debacle and then our disastrous dinner date. I don't know how she'll react when she sees me."

"You apologized for shouting at her," Robin says. "I don't remember her reciprocating. How much more inappropriate does it get than showing pictures of the previous daughter-in-law's wedding dress at your future daughter-in-law's dress fitting?"

I twirl a piece of pasta around my fork. "She was way out of line. The problem is that Shana's dead, so every time I complain I feel like a heel."

"You have every right to be upset. Laura is completely tactless—deliberately so."

I take a long sip of my wine. "She's constantly comparing me to Shana. She told me at her birthday party that I should tone it down because I couldn't hit a note. Supposedly, Shana was a virtuoso when it came to music. She also had the perfect figure because she was a fitness instructor and avid jogger, as Laura likes to remind me."

"And look where that got her," Robin says, throwing me a loaded look.

I push my pasta around the bowl, my appetite rapidly disappearing at the allusion to Shana's gruesome demise. She disappeared on a mountain path she often jogged in the early hours. Her remains were discovered a few months later, ravaged by wild animals. The police surmised that she lost her footing and fell to her death. It was tragic, and I'm sure she was a wonderful person, but I don't want to live with her ghost in my marriage.

Robin clears away the dishes and loads the dishwasher while I finish my glass of wine. She sorts through the mail and hands me mine. I discard the marketing flyers and set aside a couple of bills to pay. Opening a small white envelope, I pull out a card and read the handwritten message inside.

A secret will be revealed tomorrow. Will it be yours?

5

———————

"What's this?" I ask, handing the card to my sister. "Is it some kind of game we're playing tomorrow?"

Robin reads the card and frowns. "I'm not in charge of games. That was Martina."

She reaches for her mail and shuffles through it. "Oh, I got one too." She rips open the envelope and reads the message inside. "It's the same thing. I guess it must be some kind of a game." She grins across at me. "Hope Martina doesn't reveal anything too embarrassing."

"I'll call her right now and find out." I grab my phone and dial her number.

"Hey, bride-to-be," Martina answers. "Looking forward to your shower tomorrow?"

"I think so. Depends on what this game is all about."

"What game?"

"Oh please. You're in charge of the games, right?"

"Yes. And you're not supposed to know anything about them. Has someone been leaking my classified plans?"

"No, nothing like that. Robin and I got your cards about the secret to be revealed."

There's a long silence before Martina responds. "I have no idea what you're talking about."

A flicker of unease goes through me. "Check your mail. See if you got a card too." I put my phone on speaker and pour myself a glass of water while I wait.

A couple of minutes later, Martina comes back on the line. "Yeah, I got one. I don't understand. You asked me to handle the games."

My gaze swerves across the table to connect with Robin. What if this isn't a game? Could Laura be behind it? What secret could she possibly be talking about spilling? Goosebumps prick the back of my neck. Is she planning some kind of ambush to humiliate me in front of all my friends?

"Let me call around and see if anyone else got a card," Martina says.

I hang up and run my hands through my hair. "I feel sick," I moan to Robin. "If Laura sabotages my bridal shower tomorrow, I'm going to kill her."

"That's a drastic step. Let's not jump the gun," Robin soothes. "This might just be a fun game one of the other bridesmaids dreamed up. It's a cute little card with a heart on the front—hardly the kind of thing someone would send if they didn't have good intentions."

"You don't know Chad's mother like I do," I say. "Masking hostility is a specialty of hers."

Robin picks her card back up and studies it. "Does it look like her handwriting?"

"No, but that doesn't mean anything. She would have disguised it if it were her. She might even have paid someone else to write the cards, for all I know."

Robin rips the card in two and tosses it on the table. "My advice—just ignore it. I'm going to run the bride-to-be a bubble bath, and I want you to soak and relax, and drink more wine, and forget all about crotchety old Laura Turner. Tomorrow, you're going to have the most fabulous shower ever, and you'll have a garrison of women around you. If Laura threatens in any way to spoil things, I'll personally escort her off the premises."

I flash my sister a grateful smile. "Thanks for having my back, Robin."

After a long hot bubble bath, I'm feeling a lot more relaxed and actually beginning to look forward to my shower tomorrow—not to mention the wedding. I can't wait to set up house with Chad. We've put in an offer on a new build as neither of us wanted to live in Chad's old house with all the memories of Shana—another decision Laura expressed her disapproval of.

I towel off and put on some cozy pajamas, then go back downstairs to watch TV with Robin. We're halfway through an episode of our current crime series when my phone begins to ring. I fumble behind the cushions to look for it. "It's Martina again," I say, sliding my finger across the screen.

Robin reaches for the remote and hits pause.

"Sorry it took me so long to get back to you," Martina says. "I was waiting on a few callbacks. Turns out everyone in the bridal party got a card—you, me, Robin, Brandy, and Cindi."

"So, this isn't a game," I say, thinking out loud.

"Well, if it is, none of us know anything about it," Martina replies. "We're all a bit shook up about it, to be honest."

I scrunch my eyes shut. If it's not a game, then someone's out to sabotage my shower. It's not hard to guess who.

6

"Laura is behind this," I say through gritted teeth.

Robin shoots me an alarmed look. "You don't really think she would pull a stunt like this after what happened at the dress fitting, do you?"

I let out a snort of disgust. "Of course she would. She's shameless."

"Call her up and ask her," Robin says. "Preempt any sabotage she's plotting."

"There's no point. She'll deny it." I sink back against the couch cushions and close my eyes. "What if she embarrasses one of my guests? She'll do anything to spoil the shower. Maybe I should call the whole thing off."

"It's just a malicious attempt to put you on edge," Robin replies. "Don't worry, I won't let her spoil the shower. If she says one thing out of line, I'll kick her out."

Robin spends the rest of the evening trying to talk me out of canceling the shower. When I go to bed, it takes me longer than usual to fall asleep, and, when I do, I see Laura's shriveled lips moving at warped speed as she launches a smear campaign against me in front of all my guests.

. . .

DRESSED in the scalloped floral appliqué dress Robin and Martina helped me pick out weeks earlier, I do a twirl in front of the full-length mirror on the back of my bathroom door. Robin has expertly curled my ordinarily unmanageable hair and piled it on top of my head, leaving a few tendrils to frame my face.

"Fabulous! You're glowing," she says, hanging on my arm and beaming alongside me into the mirror. "Chad's a lucky guy."

I grimace. "Yes, he is. With a mother like his, it's a miracle he managed to rope anyone into marrying him."

"Forget about her," Robin says, massaging my shoulders. "Let all that tension out. This afternoon is all about you. Your friends are on call to squish any attempt by Laura to steal the limelight. Now, get in the car. It's showtime."

FORTY-FIVE MINUTES LATER, we pull up outside Silverbrook Manor, an exquisite country estate with lush landscaping, ornamental shrubs, topiary, and sweeping manicured lawns. Brandy, Martina, and Cindi—my childhood friend who has traveled from out of state for the shower—are already inside putting the final touches to the decor and refreshments.

"This place is unbelievable!" I gush, as I hug each of them in turn. "And the food looks incredible." I run an approving eye over the caprese skewers, stuffed mushrooms, shrimp cocktail, mini quiches, salad station, and cupcake tower—all my favorite things to eat. The briny tang of tears prickles my nose. My friends have gone all out for this occasion, and I'm so appreciative of their thoughtfulness. It's been hard dealing with Laura and her never-ending barrage of negativity and rejection. The effort my friends have gone to is like a warm hug in contrast.

The expansive great room is exquisitely decorated in dreamy champagne and rose tones, with candles flickering in floral centerpieces at each table. A tufted throne-like chair sits at one end of the room beneath an elaborate balloon arch with a bride-to-be banner backdrop. I can't help grinning from ear to ear. Robin's right. There's not much Laura can do to steal the limelight at my bridal shower. She's not the one who's going to be sitting in that chair, wrapped in a golden bride-to-be sash.

One by one, my guests arrive carrying gift bags and chattering excitedly about the stunning setting that has everyone's jaws dropping in awe—everyone, that is, except Laura.

One of the last to arrive, she bustles into the room, fanning herself. "That was such a long drive out of my way to get here. I've been suffering from shortness of breath lately, and I don't like to drive too far. I don't know why we couldn't have—"

"Mom!" Brandy cuts in. "Let me show you to your table so you can set your purse down." She winks at me over her shoulder as she whisks her mother off to her seat.

Robin arches a brow at me. "See, I told you! We're going to be on her like electric fly zappers."

Cindi glides over to me and hands me a champagne flute. "Martina's gathering everyone up to begin the games. She wants us all to head over to the couches."

"All right, everyone," Martina calls out. "Let's get started. I'm going to pass around some childhood photos of the bride and groom, and you have to guess their age in each of them."

There's a collective groan from the group, followed by plenty of good-natured banter, as everyone claims to be terrible at guessing people's ages while feverishly competing to win the prize of a vanilla scented candle.

As the shower unfolds, I gradually begin to relax. Maybe it's the second glass of champagne, or maybe it's the fact that nothing ever came of the stupid cards with the *secret to be revealed*. I'm still convinced my mother-in-law was behind it, but it was probably just a nasty dig to make me feel uneasy, as Robin said.

After we've exhausted our appetite for Mad Libs Bridal Trivia and several other hilarious games Martina has dreamed up, we move to the tables for lunch. Robin has thoughtfully seated Laura as far away from me as possible. I'm given the honor of going first in the buffet line, and I avail of the opportunity to pile my plate with all the delicious-looking finger foods.

I'm deep in conversation with Cindi when someone taps me on the shoulder. I spin around and startle at the sight of Laura. Her hand holding her glass of red wine jerks, and I watch as the crimson liquid arcs through the air and streaks down the front of my snow-white dress.

7

I yelp as I attempt to sidestep, too late to stem the tide of the velvety red contents of my mother-in-law's wine glass from streaming down my dress.

"Oh no! Look what you've done, dear," Laura cries, setting her glass down on the table. "At least you didn't break it. The glass might have cut me."

I glare at her, pressing my lips into a thin line. "You did that on purpose."

Laura tinkles a hollow laugh. "*I* did it? You're the one who bumped me."

"You could at least apologize," Cindi says, dipping her napkin in her water glass and dabbing in vain at the stain. "You've ruined her dress."

I swallow the lump in my throat, trying not to burst into tears—I'm sure that's exactly the response Laura is hoping for. Instead, I accompany Cindi to the bathroom to assess the damage.

"There's no getting that stain out," I tell her, twisting sideways to view myself in the mirror. "You guys will just have to take pictures of me from the other side to hide it."

"What a witch that woman is," Cindi fumes. "I can have Brandy make her leave, if you want."

"No," I say, smoothing out my dress as best I can. I take a deep breath, steeling myself to rise above Laura's pathetic attempt to humiliate me. "If I banish her, she'll play the martyr, and then Chad will have to listen to her endless whining about it. It will be more of a punishment for her to watch me sit on my tufted throne and open my gifts. Let's get back out there and have some fun."

Seated in my gilded chair, with my bride-to-be sash angled to cover the stain on my dress, my stomach flutters in anticipation. Robin hands each gift to me while Martina jots down who it's from and what it is. I can't help noting with satisfaction that Laura looks thoroughly displeased that I'm enjoying myself instead of sobbing in the bathroom.

"I love these decorative seagrass baskets, Cindi!" I say, eagerly passing her gift around for everyone to admire. I can't wait to show Chad all the gorgeous home accessories, kitchen gadgets, and linens we've received to set up our new home.

My shoulders tense when Robin hands me a gift bag from Laura. I'm going to have to simper and thank her, while inwardly seething about the fact that she ruined my dress. Trying not to show my resentment, I pull the tissue out of the bag and reach for the gift inside. I hold it up and stare in horror at the hideous crocheted blanket in the vilest green wool imaginable.

"I made it myself," Laura announces, the slash of lipstick on her pale face twisting into a proud smile.

I can't bring myself to lie, and tell her I love it, but I can hardly tell her how I really feel about it either. "Um, thank you, Laura. I can ... only imagine the amount of work that was."

"Hold it up for everyone to see, dear," Laura says, a flicker of impatience crossing her face.

There's a subdued chorus of faltering sentiments, but I don't hear any real enthusiasm for the ugly blanket. The worst thing about it is that I won't be able to get rid of it now that she claims to have made it.

Laura claps her hands to get everyone's attention. "I'd like to make a short speech, if I may, as the matriarch of the shower. Many of you knew my precious daughter-in-law, Shana. No one can ever replace her, and we all miss her dreadfully, but, understandably, my son doesn't want to be alone for the rest of his life, and he has chosen to remarry." She smirks at me. "Lucky girl." She clears her throat and continues, "I look forward to welcoming some Turner grandchildren in the not-too-distant future." She wiggles her eyebrows at me. "Unless you have any breaking news on that front, dear. I couldn't help but notice how you filled out that wedding dress when you tried it on."

I hear a sharp intake of breath as all eyes swerve to me.

"You'll be the first to hear about it when that day comes," I reply, lying through my teeth. She'll be the last person I'll share that news with.

"Well, that is a relief. I hate to see a good man trapped into marriage."

Shocked murmuring ripples around the room.

Robin raises her brows at me and inclines her head toward the door, inviting me to take her up on her promise to haul Laura out of here.

I give a subtle shake of my head. I won't give Laura the satisfaction of knowing she got under my skin. I have other ways of dealing with her.

"Okay, let's open your next gift, Eva," Robin cuts in.

I let out a silent breath, thankful to be moving on from Laura's ghastly gift and scathing speech.

"Pass my blanket around, first," Laura interrupts. "It's a very intricate pattern which you can only see close up. It took hours of work, and I know everyone will want to feel how soft the wool is."

I refrain from responding, leaving Robin to handle the situation. I don't want to come across as the disgruntled daughter-in-law, even though I'm fairly certain Laura didn't make the blanket herself. I've never seen or heard of her crocheting, or knitting, or sewing anything. It doesn't even look new. It's probably something she found in a thrift store and decided to pass off as her own.

Robin pulls the blanket back out of the gift bag and passes it to Cindi. I watch as it moves around the circle, and everyone gives it an obligatory once-over. When it comes back to Robin, she stuffs it unceremoniously into the gift bag and sets it aside.

Laura beams around at the group. "I always think a handmade gift is so much more thoughtful."

"All right," Robin says, ignoring Laura's last comment as she reaches for a large pink envelope. "This one's not attached to a gift. Not sure who it's from."

"Let's find out," I say, tearing open the envelope.

The blood in my veins turns to ice when I read the card inside.

8

I reread the card, acid swirling up from my stomach.

Guess who's having an affair with someone at work?

Below the text is a mug shot of me clutching a slate displaying my booking number and name. A nerve twitches in my neck and a thorny prickling sensation creeps up my spine. How can something this twisted be happening at my bridal shower?

"Who's the card from?" Robin asks, trying to peer over my shoulder.

My fingers tremble as I hand it to her. Is this the secret that was to be revealed? Except it's a lie. I'm not having an affair with somebody at work—or anyone, for that matter. This has to be another one of Laura's sick stunts.

Robin snaps the card shut and shoots me a grim look. " I'll get rid of it," she mutters, slipping it into a bag of trash by her feet.

Martina raises a brow, pen poised to make a note of the gift giver's name. "Everything all right?"

"Aren't you going to pass the card around?" Laura calls out, sounding peeved. "We all want to read it."

"It's just some mail that got mixed up with the shower gifts," Robin replies, forcing a smile.

I open several more gifts in a trance, going through the motions of smiling and thanking people, but my mind won't stop racing. The card must be from Laura—who else would do something so malicious? She was eager for me to pass it around for everyone to see. No doubt, she wants the rumor mill she started about me on social media to keep going. I'm proud of myself for not playing into her hands and making a scene over the stupid card—it might only entice her to ruin my wedding day too. Once Chad and I are safely married, all bets are off. I won't hesitate to call her out to her face on all her petty, insufferable ways and passive-aggressive behavior. For now, at least, I've foiled her plans to reveal a secret about me that was nothing more than a boldfaced lie.

Robin reaches for a beautifully wrapped parcel tied with a white satin ribbon and hands it to me. "No card with this one that I can see."

"Who's this from?" I ask, glancing around the group.

The women look at one another, eyebrows raised, shrugging their shoulders.

"A few people who couldn't make it to the shower mailed their gifts," Martina says.

"I know our aunts all mailed gifts, but I'm not sure who that one's from," Robin responds, frowning. "I don't remember bringing it with me. Maybe there's a card inside."

I tear open the gold and white paper to reveal a long narrow box with a familiar crest on the outside.

"Awesome!" I say. "It's the carving knife I had on my registry." I lift off the lid and remove the tissue paper.

A scream reverberates around the room, and it takes me a minute to realize it's me.

9

I shove the box containing the bloody knife out of my lap as hard as I can, and leap to my feet. The knife clatters to the floor and skids to a stop next to a pile of gifts, glinting defiantly up at me. Everyone's talking at once, the expressions on their faces morphing into shock and horror as it becomes clear what was in the box. The atmosphere in the room has taken a dark turn, and the cacophony of distressed voices is making me nauseous. I'm vaguely aware of Robin taking me by the arm and helping me back to my chair.

"Sit tight," she orders me. "I'm going to fetch you a glass of ice water."

I drop my head into my hands in an attempt to stop the room from spinning around me. Someone must have disposed of the knife because it's no longer lying at my feet winking belligerently up at me. Now that I've had a few minutes to process it, I realize it couldn't have been dried blood. It was far too bright for that—more likely paint or ketchup. This was a sick prank designed to cast a shadow on my special day. After a moment or two, my racing heart begins to slow, and the ache in my chest dissipates.

Robin returns with a glass of water and stands over me while I drink it. I blink myself back to the moment, vaguely aware that my guests have dispersed and are standing in small groups of two and three around the room conducting hushed conversations.

I groan out loud. How am I supposed to continue on with the shower after this? I just want to go home. But some of the woman might feel slighted if I don't open their gifts.

I hand Robin back the glass. "Where's the knife?" I ask, in a tremulous tone.

"Martina took care of it."

"Was there a card inside?"

Robin lowers her voice. "A note: *beware the killer among you.*"

My eyes widen in shock. Is Laura threatening me? Or is she trying to convince people I'm a killer? I've been pretty vocal about how much I'd like to make her disappear permanently, but it was just talk.

"Do you want me to call the police?" Robin asks. "This feels like a real threat. No one here knows who was behind it."

I grimace. "No. It's just a cruel joke to ruin my shower. And we both know who's behind it. Let's try and get things back on track, we'll deal with this afterward. People have made an effort to travel all the way here. I don't want to send them home without opening the rest of the gifts. We haven't even had dessert yet."

"If that's what you want to do," Robin replies with a reluctant sigh. "I'll have Martina help round everyone up."

I sink back down in my chair, trying to stop myself from shaking. I watch as Robin and Martina go around the room talking to the women, presumably reassuring them that this was some kind of tasteless prank. One by one, they file back to their seats. I brace myself for Laura's return, determined to stare her down and let her know her stupid plans to ruin my day have not succeeded.

"Okay, ladies," Robin says, beaming around at everyone. "We had an unexpected interruption, but we're going to put all the unpleasantness behind us and move forward opening the rest of the gifts and enjoying that yummy dessert station."

The women exchange hesitant smiles as they settle back into their seats.

"I don't know where Mom went," Brandy says, peering over her shoulder. "She must have gone to the bathroom."

"We don't need to wait on her," I say to Martina. "The last thing I'm going to do is accommodate her after this latest stunt."

My guests do their best to reignite the excitement and anticipation from earlier, but it's obvious the mood in the room has taken a hit. I suspect most of the woman will be relieved when the shower ends, and they can take their leave. I don't blame them. This was a creepy turn of events despite whatever reassurances Robin and Martina gave them.

It's only when I've finished opening all my gifts, and everyone has drifted over to the dessert station that I realize Laura never returned.

"Has anyone seen Laura?" I ask.

"Brandy's gone to look for her," Martina replies.

"Maybe she got spooked after she saw the bloody knife and she's hiding from the killer," Robin says with a sarcastic grin.

I let out a derisive snort. "Not likely, if she's the one

behind it. She's probably disappointed I didn't freak out and cut the shower short. Knowing her, she went home in a huff after not getting the response she wanted."

"What a selfish cow!" Robin mutters. "She could at least have had the decency to say goodbye."

A moment later, Brandy comes bustling back into the room, a strained expression on her face.

"Did you find your mom?" Robin asks.

"No. I've looked all throughout the house," Brandy replies. "I'm starting to get worried. She's here somewhere because her purse is on her chair and her car's still parked in the driveway. She was all freaked out about the bloody knife, and complaining of shortness of breath again. She might have gone outside to get some fresh air and passed out. We're going to need to search the grounds."

My mood immediately plummets. I should have known Laura would raise the stakes if she didn't get the reaction she wanted. She couldn't destroy my shower with her malicious stunts, so she's decided to steal the limelight by disappearing.

10

W ord quickly spreads that Laura has gone missing, and the guests abandon the dessert station en masse to help look for her.

"She was complaining about feeling winded when she arrived," Brandy says, her brow rumpled in worry. "She might have stepped outside to get some fresh air."

"Let's split up into pairs and search the grounds," Robin suggests. Her concerned eyes rake my face. "You don't have to come, Sis. You look really pale yourself."

"I'm fine," I retort, averting my gaze. The truth is, I feel like all the blood has drained from my head. Laura just upped the ante and took a hatchet to my bridal shower. All people will remember about it now is the bloody knife, and the fact that my mother-in-law went missing. She got her way in the end, despite my best efforts not to cave in the face of her sabotage. I don't understand why she hates me so much—is it just because I'm nothing like the beautiful and accomplished Shana? Or is there something more to it than that?

Robin and I head out across the back lawns and begin

traipsing through the ornamental gardens to the fruit orchards beyond. My white sandals will be filthy after this, not that it matters—my dress is already ruined, and the shower is a bust now anyway.

"It's a deliberate ploy on her part," I rage. "She's probably hiding someplace, waiting until we're all frantic before she makes a dramatic reentrance."

Robin throws me a dubious look. "There's a chance she's passed out somewhere. She was complaining during the shower about her heart beating erratically and feeling lightheaded. And she was visibly shaken when you opened the box with that bloody knife. I know you think she was behind it, but she seemed genuinely terrified when she found out what was in the note."

I toss my head. "All an act. I'll bet anything she's the one who wrote it and planted the knife. She just didn't get the reaction she wanted, which is why she's resorted to this pathetic vanishing act. It's the final nail in the coffin of my shower."

"If you're right, you should give some serious consideration to calling off the wedding," Robin says. "Or at least postponing it. You can't live like this. If Chad's not willing to sever all ties with his crazy mother, then he's not worth fighting for."

I plod along, ruminating on the truth of what Robin is telling me for the umpteenth time. I don't want to be miserable for the rest of my life. I need to have a heart-to-heart with Chad and make it clear that I don't want anything more to do with his mother. If he's unwilling to honor my wishes, it might be the end of the road for us.

I'm startled out of my morbid thoughts by the sound of shouting.

"They must have found her," Robin says, breaking into a run.

I hobble along behind her as best I can in my grass-stained heels. The others have converged on a large greenhouse at the far end of an expansive vegetable garden. Brandy is kneeling down on the ground, surrounded by the other women who are all fussing over a dramatically dazed and confused-looking Laura.

"Should I call for an ambulance?" Cindi asks.

"No! Please don't fuss over me," Laura says, in the kind of pitiful tone that begs everyone to do exactly that. "I just needed to take a short walk to clear my head. I must have passed out—I tend to struggle with low blood sugar in the afternoons."

"Let's get you back inside the house," Brandy says. Assisted by Martina, she helps her mother to her feet. Laura catches sight of my disheveled appearance, and a smirk crosses her face before she quickly masks it. I glower back at her. I'm not going to pretend to offer her sympathy for this ridiculous stunt she pulled on herself.

Back in the house, all the attention is still firmly centered on Laura. The women find a wet rag for her forehead, fetch her a bottle of water, and bring her a sweet treat for her low blood sugar—a condition I didn't know she suffered from until a few minutes ago.

"What a distressing function this has turned out to be," Laura moans, pressing the rag to her forehead in an exaggerated fashion.

"That's an understatement," I snap, folding my arms in front of me. "I wonder whose fault that is. Let's think for a minute about who here would be most likely to want to spoil this day."

Laura blinks innocently up at me. "I know you're upset about that nasty prank with the knife, dear, but there's nothing to be gained by throwing a tantrum. It was probably one of the groomsmen. You know what pranksters they are." She turns to her daughter. "Brandy, be a dear and help me to the bathroom."

As she wanders off, I hear her mutter, "I wouldn't be surprised if Eva planted that knife herself."

"Why would she do that?" Brandy asks.

"That's what everyone here should be asking themselves. She's said it herself—she wants to kill me."

11

Four Weeks Later

Robin and I are getting ready to head to the church for the wedding rehearsal, followed by dinner at my favorite Italian restaurant—the same place Chad took me to the night he proposed. I survey myself in the mirror, cringing when I see the mottled bags beneath my eyes. I've done the best I can to conceal them with make up, but there's no disguising the fact that I haven't been sleeping well in the run up to the wedding.

After the unmitigated disaster of a bridal shower, I've lowered my expectations for the wedding. Chad and I have had several heated conversations about it, and I've had to resign myself to the fact that, like it or not, Laura is going to be attending our wedding. The only consolation is that it's the last time I'll have to interact with her. After some tough negotiations, Chad has promised to honor my wish to cut off all contact with her after we're married. For his part, I've given him my blessing to meet up with his mother for the occasional lunch or coffee date, if he wants to continue the relationship.

"Ready?" Robin asks, beaming at me as she sticks her head into my bedroom.

"Coming." I sling the strap of my purse over my shoulder and follow her out to the car.

"I can't believe it's the day before your wedding," Robin says, as she backs down the driveway. "It feels surreal."

"It's also the first time I'll be setting eyes on you know who since the shower," I say in a distinctly unenthusiastic tone.

"Ignore her. You don't have to interact with her."

"I still can't believe she told Brandy I wanted to kill her."

Robin arches an amused brow. "She wasn't entirely wrong on that count."

I give a mirthless laugh. "There's a difference between wishing someone dead and doing something about it. I'm dreading having to stand next to her for wedding photographs. I'll go through the motions, but you'd better believe I won't be ordering any pictures with her in them."

"Maybe just one for your dartboard," Robin says with a wink.

My spirit deflates even further when we pull up at the church and I see Laura's car parked outside. I suppose it's better than her arriving late and making a dramatic entrance that interrupts the rehearsal, but I was half hoping she might have forgotten all about it. Wishful thinking on my part. She's not going to miss an opportunity to gaze adoringly at her son, while staring daggers at me.

"You got this," Robin says to me as we're walking in. "Chin up."

Chad's face lights up the minute he sees me. He hurries down the aisle and pulls me in for a kiss. "Ready to become Mrs. Turner?" he asks, a note of pride in his voice.

A shudder runs across my shoulders. I'm not sure if it's

anticipation of what my heart wants most, or dread at the thought of sharing the same name as my mother-in-law. I cast a quick glance in her direction, but she's sitting ramrod straight with her back to me in the front pew on the groom's side of the church. She must have heard me come in, but she's making no attempt to greet me, which suits me just fine.

The bridesmaids and groomsmen eventually trickle in, and the minister starts the proceedings by welcoming everyone and explaining the order of events. After answering a few questions, we practice walking into the church, beginning with Laura leaning on Chad's arm as he escorts her to the family pew. When she unlinks her arm with his, she taps her cheek for him to kiss before taking her seat. I twist my lips in annoyance at her triumphant smile in my direction. She's making a point of letting me know the control she still exerts over him.

When it comes time for my practice walk up the aisle, I grip the bouquet of ribbons Martina made for me from the bridal shower, and wait for the minister's cue. All eyes in the bridal party are on me as I step into the aisle. I pull my shoulders back and hold my head high, taking slow, measured steps. I suck in a steadying breath, focusing all my attention on Chad who's waiting at the front of the church, smiling lovingly at me. The emotion of the moment wells up inside me and tears prickle my eyes—tears of happiness for the love I feel for my husband-to-be, and tears of sadness that my parents won't be here to share this special day with me. I brush my damp lashes with the back of my hand, and try to picture myself tomorrow, the train of my wedding gown rustling behind me as light spills through the stained glass windows.

That's when I hear the thud of a body falling to the floor.

12

Instantly, the idyllic moment is shattered. Pandemonium erupts as everyone breaks rank and runs toward the pew where Laura was sitting. Chad is no longer staring adoringly back at me. Even the minister has turned his attention to the woman who has once again decided to rob me of what should have been one of my most cherished memories, second only to the big day itself. I stand seething in the middle of the aisle, watching as the woman I hate the most in the entire world is surrounded by everyone I love the most. Nothing about this moment is fair. I know I should try to control my anger, but everything inside me wants to burst forth and right this wrong.

Breathing hard, I stomp the rest of the way up the aisle and over to where Laura is laying on the floor being fanned by several orders of service. She sits up slowly, groaning. " Can someone fetch me some water."

"Happy to," I say through gritted teeth. I snatch up a bottle from the pew, unscrew the lid, and pour the contents over her head.

"Eva!" Chad cries out, grabbing the bottle from me. " What's got into you?"

"I think the question you should be asking is what's got into *her*," I fling back at him. "She simply can't stand the fact that we're getting married, and she's determined to ruin everything she can."

Without giving him a chance to respond, I hurl my ribbon bouquet to the ground, whirl around, and tromp back down the aisle.

"Eva! Wait!" Chad calls after me.

Ignoring him, I increase my pace. I'm tired of watching him pick the wrong side when it comes to choosing between me and his mother.

Robin runs to catch up with me. "Wait! I'm coming with you. We need to talk about this."

"I'm not in the mood to talk," I growl, exiting the church and marching across the parking lot to the car.

"Eva, please," Robin cajoles. "You can't abandon your own rehearsal. What about the dinner? Everything's already been paid for."

"Unlock the car, please. I'm not going to dinner with that woman."

"She probably won't even be there now. She just fainted. Chad will likely have to drop her home."

Cindi and Martina come jogging across the parking lot toward us.

"Eva, please don't go," Martina says, panting from exertion. "Chad can put his mom in an Uber and send her home. We can still finish up the rehearsal and go to dinner afterward."

"What's the point?" I say grumpily. "She'll likely pull the same stunt tomorrow and ruin the actual ceremony. She's the most vindictive, maniacal person I know."

"She fainted, that's all," Cindi says. "It was stuffy in there, to be honest."

I shake my head in disbelief. "I can't believe she has you fooled. Do you really think she passed out at the exact moment I was coming down the aisle?"

I throw a quick glance at the church door. If Chad cared one iota, he would come after me. Instead he's in there taking care of his mother after her award-winning performance.

I tug my hands through the hair Robin styled so carefully earlier. "Even if she doesn't come to the dinner, my stomach is curdled at this point. I don't think I could eat a thing."

"You can't let her win," Robin says, taking my hands in hers. "How about I tell Chad that you're only going to come back inside and go to the rehearsal dinner if she goes home? At least give him the chance to do the right thing and prove whose side he's really on."

I let out a heavy sigh, letting my shoulders sag. "Fine. But I'm not going to get dragged into a back-and-forth argument about it. He either abides by my wishes or the dinner is off. Maybe the wedding too."

Robin turns to Martina. "Can you relay the message and let us know what he says?"

She chews on her lip. "Um, sure ... I guess."

She walks slowly back to the church door. I know this isn't what she signed up for when she agreed to be one of my bridesmaids. I don't blame her for dragging her heels. My future mother-in-law won't hesitate to bite the head off the messenger if she doesn't like the message.

I turn to Cindi. "What happened in there after I left?"

Her eyebrows rise a touch. "As you can imagine, Laura was none too happy about her unexpected baptism."

"She asked for water," I answer with a shrug.

"She's saying you assaulted her. Martina and I said we would try to talk you into coming back inside and apologizing."

"I'm not going to apologize to her," I say.

Cindi twists her hands in front of her. "I think the minister is expecting you to. After all, you still want him to marry you and Chad tomorrow."

I let out a heavy sigh. "I suppose everyone else thinks I overreacted too."

"They're willing to show a stressed-out bride a little grace, and you deserve more than most with everything you've had to put up with."

"I'd be a hypocrite if I apologized," I say. "She deserved what she got, and worse, for pulling another stunt."

"You're making a judgment call without any evidence— you don't know for sure that she did it deliberately. What if she really does have low blood sugar?" Cindi pauses, her expression softening. "You do want to marry Chad, don't you? If you walk away now, you might never get the chance."

The finality of her words hits me like a thunderbolt. "Fine, I'll go back in. But not until that Uber arrives, because if I get within a few feet of her, there's no telling what I'll do."

13

I wait in Robin's car until the Uber drives off with the wicked witch in tow. Afterward, I go back inside the church and make a point of apologizing to the minister for my explosive temper, because I do need to make sure he shows up tomorrow, or else Laura has won. He graciously takes it in his stride—I'm guessing he's experienced his fair share of emotional outbursts from bridal parties in one form or another over the years.

Thankfully, the rest of the rehearsal goes off without a hitch, and by the time we get to the restaurant, the mood has taken a turn for the better. Without Laura to put a damper on things, we let loose and enjoy our chargrilled steaks, specialty cocktails, and a fabulous dessert station, before pulling on our coats to head home.

"See you at the aisle, Mrs. Turner-to-be," Chad says, kissing me softly on the lips.

I flinch, despite the tenderness of the moment. I used to love how smoothly *Ava Turner* rolled off the tongue, but lately there's a sour twist to it. Is there nothing Laura can't pollute in her noxious wake?

Despite my misgivings about marrying into the Turner family, I fall into a deep sleep and wake feeling rested the following morning.

"Today's the day, sleepyhead," Robin chirps, bringing me a coffee in bed. "I'm making us omelettes. According to the infinite wisdom of the internet, the bride should have a protein filled breakfast."

I laugh as I accept the mug she hands me. "What time are the rest of the bridesmaids going to be here?"

"Around nine-thirty. Make up and hair begins at ten."

"And the mimosas?"

Robin quirks an eyebrow. "The minute the girls get here."

I sip my coffee, savoring every mouthful, mindful that this is my last caffeine rush as Eva Boucher. Despite my euphoria at the day finally being here, I can't shake a niggling feeling of unease in my belly. The rehearsal dinner last night was relaxing without the threat of Laura's histrionics hanging over it, but today doesn't promise any such relief. What if she stands up in the middle of the ceremony and protests our union? Martina has promised to body slam her if she does, but the ceremony will still be spoiled if they have to drag her kicking and screaming out of the church.

The remainder of my bridal party trickles in and soon we're sipping mimosas as the makeup artist and hairdresser weave their magic. I'm delighted to see that the makeup artist has seemingly erased any remaining shadows beneath my eyes. I actually look as refreshed as I feel inside.

"Thank you! You've done a fantastic job," I say as I vacate the chair for Brandy and move over to the hairdressing station for the next round of my makeover.

Brandy's phone begins to ring and she jumps up, frowning. "Be right back," she says, pulling an apologetic face to the makeup artist who's poised with foundation brush in hand.

"Everything all right?" I ask her when she resumes her seat.

Her forehead creases. "That was Chad. He can't get a hold of Mom."

My stomach twists as though my intestines are being wrung out like a wet rag.

"I tried calling her too, but she didn't answer," Brandy goes on. "I left her a message to call me back. Chad's going to swing by her house if she doesn't respond in the next thirty minutes or so."

My jaw drops. "You've got to be kidding me, Brandy. Chad's got enough on his plate this morning without having to drive over to your mother's. You know why she's doing this. She's just trying to ruin the day."

Brandy grimaces. "I'm sorry, Eva. I don't know what to tell you. She's still our mother—we have to make sure nothing's happened to her."

Martina and Cindi exchange a loaded glance. The last thing any of us want is to have to drop everything and go looking for Laura again. To be perfectly honest, nothing would thrill me more than for her to miss the wedding.

I reach for my mimosa and take a generous swig, trying to revive the excitement I felt before Chad called. I'm convinced Laura's fine and simply up to her old tricks, but I can understand his need to make sure she's okay. I just hope the antics don't continue after we're married. My patience with her petty, vindictive ways has worn thin, and I don't relish the idea of my husband constantly being on call to cater to her every whim.

The morning slips by with increasingly uneasy updates from Chad. Neither he nor Brandy has been able to get ahold of Laura. The mood is notably strained as we attempt to stay focused on the wedding and avoid talking about the elephant in the room.

The hours tick by until we're down to forty-five minutes before the ceremony begins. I dial Chad's number, steeling myself for bad news.

"Heard anything?" I ask.

"Nothing. I don't know what to do."

"She'll probably show up at the church, thrilled with herself for making us all worry needlessly."

"What if she doesn't?" Chad responds. "I have to call the police. She wouldn't miss the wedding unless something had happened."

I let a long silence unfold before I respond. "We're going ahead with the wedding regardless, Chad. It's either her or me."

14

The atmosphere in the limo on the drive to the church is tense. Brandy is texting furiously back-and-forth with Chad as they continue to reach out to friends, relatives, and neighbors in the hope that someone heard or saw something of their mother. Cindy and Martina are engaged in a hushed conversation behind their hands, presumably discussing how they're going to handle things if Laura makes a late appearance and inter-rupts the proceedings by objecting to our union—which is still my biggest fear. Robin keeps up a steady stream of banal chatter with me, trying, and failing, to take my mind off the fact that my devious mother-in-law has managed to steal the limelight once more by marking herself absent.

I can't help wondering how much time Chad has had to get ready for our upcoming nuptials. Given the fact that his mother is missing, I suspect his focus has been diverted. It's a brilliant ploy on Laura's part. Whether or not she shows up to the ceremony, she's already derailed the morning and soured any anticipation of our wedding. Chad actually suggested postponing it until later this evening, but I vetoed the idea. I'm convinced his mother will show up when she's good and ready—dressed in white, no doubt, to spite me.

"Here we are," Robin says, as we pull up outside the church. She climbs out of the limo first and helps me gather up my dress. I'm soon swept up in the commotion as my bridesmaids and I pose for pictures just outside the church before lining up to make our grand entrance. My bouquet is shaking in my hands. I'm not nervous to get married, I'm nervous of Laura showing up to disrupt things.

"Are you sure you still want to walk down the aisle alone?" Robin asks, eying my trembling fingers. "I can walk alongside you, if you like."

"Thanks, but I want to do it just the way we planned it," I say firmly. "Mom and Dad will be with me in spirit."

Robin nods and gets in line in front of me at the behest of the wedding coordinator.

When the music begins, my heartbeat accelerates. It feels like a clarion call to Laura to fly in on her broomstick. Before I realize what's happening, I've entered the church and I'm walking down the aisle. Each step feels weightier than the last. I swallow the hard lump in my throat and try to focus on Chad standing at the front of the church, hands clasped in front of him.

Halfway up the aisle, I cast a quick glance over the sea of faces on either side of me. I'm greeted by strained smiles and curious eyes. Everyone must know by now that Chad's mother is missing. Do they think I'm an awful daughter-in-law for insisting on going ahead with the wedding?

I turn my attention back to the man I love—handsome in his gray suit and crisp white shirt, freshly shaven with neatly combed hair. My emotions circle in a whirlwind inside my chest. Hope mingled with dread. Joy and gloom. Love mixed with hate. I feel like I'm at war with myself. I want so much to be happy in this moment, but I'm doubting the monumental step I'm about to take. Instead of fulfilling my dream of becoming Mrs. Turner, I can't help wondering if I'm bidding the life I've known farewell to enter into a nightmare.

As I take my place opposite Chad, I hand my bouquet off to Robin. My eyes dart to the entryway to the church, dreading seeing Laura rear her ugly head as she darkens the door. I barely hear a word the minister says, and stumble over the vows he asks me to repeat after him. I try to bring myself back to the moment when Chad slides the wedding ring onto my finger, eyes locked on me as he faithfully promises to love and cherish me. I'm shocked when I hear the minister pronounce us husband and wife. I feel like the whole ceremony zipped by while my mind was tangled up with thoughts of Laura bursting through the door.

Before I realize what's happening, Chad's lips are on mine, and a cheer goes up from the crowd. He grabs my hand and raises my arm in a jubilant salute as we dance back down the aisle.

I should be marinating in the joy of being Mrs. Turner, but my only thought as we exit the church is where on earth the other Mrs. Turner could possibly be.

15

S eated at the head table in our banquet room at The Grand Landsby, Chad and I have our first real opportunity to talk.

"Brandy called the police to report Mom missing," he says, lowering his voice.

I roll my eyes. "I'm sure she'll love all the attention when she decides to show her face again. She'll probably waltz in here any minute now. She's hardly going to miss out on this meal after she insisted on the beef course, and the cheese-cake bites, even though she knows I hate cheesecake."

A nerve twitches in Chad's neck. "Surely it wasn't too much to let her feel like she was participating in the wedding planning. It's a petty detail in the grand scheme of things. Do you have to bring it up every time we talk about her?"

"She also mailed an invitation to your ex-girlfriend from high school," I mutter, attempting to smile at the guests walking by our table. "Did you know that? Thankfully, she declined."

Chad shrugs. "She's married now. My mom was best friends with her mom. What does it matter?"

I lift my glass of water and raise it to my lips to hide the peeved expression on my face from the roving eyes of our guests. I hate that we're having our first argument as husband and wife before we've even had a chance to toast our union. But I know who to blame for that. Even in her absence, my mother-in-law has managed to put a wedge between us.

"I'm going to the restroom," I say, reaching for my satin purse as I get to my feet.

"Don't be long. They're about to start the speeches," Chad replies.

Robin pushes back her chair. "I'll come with you."

We make our way through the sea of tables, stopping here and there to greet people, and accept congratulatory hugs and wishes.

Inside the restroom, I station myself in front of the mirror to touch up my make up.

"Any news yet?" Robin asks, as she reapplies her lipstick.

I shake my head. "Chad said Brandy reported Laura missing. I guess they didn't want to wait any longer for her to make her grand entrance."

Robin smacks her lips together. "Can't say I blame them. They would never forgive themselves if it turned out she'd had a stroke or something. Look on the bright side—you were able to enjoy the ceremony without her."

"I wish I could say I enjoyed it, but I had one eye on the door the entire time, terrified she would come blazing through it shouting out her objections. It was all over before I knew it, and I honestly don't remember a word of Chad's vows."

Robin throws me a sympathetic smile. "I guess he'll just have to read them to you later."

I grimace. "That's the other thing. If she shows up late to the reception, we're going to have to retake some of the pictures. Chad wants her in them."

"It's the last favor you'll have to do for that woman. After today, you get to part ways." Robin pauses, widening her eyes. "Unless of course she's waiting for you at your honeymoon Airbnb on the beach in Maui."

I let out an audible gasp.

Robin laughs. "Relax! I'm just teasing!"

But a finger of dread is already working its way up my spine. "You don't really think she would show up there, do you?"

"Of course not. How would she know the address?"

"It wouldn't be hard to find out. She might have stuck her nose into Chad's email when she was at his house," I say. "She has a key, and his computer's always on."

A small frown scurries across Robin's forehead. "I hardly think she'd fly all the way to Maui to crash your honeymoon. Chad's not going to let that happen."

"He can't stop it if she surprises us," I say. I groan as I grip the edge of the sink. "Now I'm going to have to sleep with one eye open on my honeymoon. I can't get that woman out of my life no matter how hard I try."

"You married into the family against my advice," Robin says in a told-you-so voice as she slips her lipstick back into her clutch. "We'd better get back out there before a rumor starts that the bride has gone missing too."

As we settle in to listen to the speeches, my thoughts start wandering again. The dark cloud of anger in my heart threatens to brew into a fully-fledged storm. My mother-in-law better not be planning to follow us to Maui.

If she does, I'll make sure she never returns.

16

When Chad gets to his feet to give his speech, I squeeze his hand encouragingly. He's not comfortable speaking in front of large crowds, and I know this is going to be even more emotional for him now that his mother's not here.

"I'd like to thank all of you for coming from near and far to celebrate this day with me and my beautiful bride, Eva. She means the world to me and I can't wait to spend the rest of my life with her."

He smiles down at me, his eyes pooling with emotion. "You look absolutely stunning, sweetheart, and I feel like the luckiest man alive to be married to you."

I blow him a kiss in return. "Right back at you."

It finally feels right to be Mrs. Turner. Despite everything his mother has done to drive us apart, we made it to the altar in the end. We're man and wife now, and nothing his mother does to thwart us from here on out will ever undo that.

"I'd like to thank my mother, Laura," Chad continues, "and my sister Brandy, for all their support through the

years—many of which were ... difficult, before I met Eva."
He chokes on the words before continuing. "Unfortunately,
my mother is unable to be with us today due to unforeseen
circumstances, but I'm sure if she were here she would raise
a glass to toast our marriage as I'm going to ask you all to do
now. Thank you for being part of our special day and here's
to a lifetime of love and laughter!"

The clink of glasses echoes around the room and shouts
of *congratulations* ring out from every corner. Chad leans
over and plants a kiss on my lips.

"You handled that perfectly," I whisper to him.

"I could hardly tell the truth and say we have no idea
where my mother is," Chad mutters back. "I don't want her
disappearance to become the topic of conversation for the
rest of the evening."

The DJ kicks the music into high gear and invites Chad
and I out onto the floor for our first dance. As I twirl around
in his arms, all the unpleasantness of the past few days
melts away. "I'm so happy, babe," I say. "You're everything I
ever dreamed of."

Chad laughs. "We've only been married how many
minutes? Give it a few more hours."

I punch him playfully on the arm as he dips me down
and kisses me again in our grand finale move. Hand-in-
hand, we return to our seats accompanied by a round of
clapping and whooping.

"And now for the mother and son dance," the DJ
announces over the speaker system.

The hum of voices dies down instantly.

"I forgot to tell him to take that out of the lineup," Chad
mutters, shifting uncomfortably in his seat.

"You'd think he would have used some common sense

after you mentioned in your speech that your mother wasn't here."

"He was probably fiddling with his equipment and not paying attention."

"It looks like Martina's having a word with him right now," I say.

Moments later, the DJ opens the dance floor up to everyone, and the party gets underway. I'm swept back into the throng of bodies by Cindi, and soon find myself dancing with the rest of my bridal party in a small group near the center of the floor. Several songs later, I look around to see Chad sitting alone at our table, head bent over his phone. I feel both sorry for him, and angry with him at the same time. He should be out here dancing and making memories —making an appearance in our wedding video.

I tug Robin's arm gently. "I'm going to go check on Chad. Be back in a minute," I yell in her ear. Grabbing my skirts, I pick my way carefully through the pulsing crowd and back to our table.

"Aren't you coming to dance with us?" I ask, slumping down in my seat and reaching for my water.

He plasters on a smile and slips his phone into his pocket. "Sure. I was just checking a message from one of Mom's neighbors."

"Any news?"

He shakes his head. "They haven't seen her since yesterday."

He reaches for my hand to drag me back onto the dance floor just as Brandy comes barreling toward us, a skittish look on her face. I register the shock in her eyes and brace myself for the worst.

17

"It's Mom!" Brandy rasps, thrusting her phone at Chad. "She finally texted me back."

Chad studies the screen for a minute, a stiff grimace on his face.

"What did she say?" I ask.

He grunts. "Doesn't matter. The important thing is that she's safe."

I hold my hand out for the phone. "It's my wedding too that she bailed on. I deserve to know what her excuse was."

With a weary sigh, Chad hands me the phone.

I read the message out loud. "You don't have to be worried about me. I'm fine. I know when I'm not wanted. I hope Eva enjoyed her special day without me."

My eyes dart from Chad to Brandy. "That's rich! She's trying to guilt-trip me for being a no-show at her own son's wedding. Not one word of apology. Talk about passive-aggressive on steroids."

Chad throws a discreet glance around. "Let's not get into it right now. The main thing is she's okay." He turns to Brandy. "Have you tried calling her?"

She nods. "She won't pick up. I texted her and asked where she is, but she didn't respond to that either."

I fold my arms in front of me. "I doubt she's roughing it on the streets. She probably booked herself into a hotel somewhere just to give us all a heart attack."

"You'd better let the police know she's okay," Chad says to Brandy.

She nods. "Will do."

Chad pulls me in close and hugs me tight. "I'm so relieved. I was terrified she might have had a stroke or something—she's been complaining about chest pains lately." He plants a kiss on the top of my head and releases me. "Let's get back out on the dance floor and show everyone our moves."

After dancing our hearts out, we collapse back in our chairs, sweaty and laughing. Knowing that Laura isn't lying in a ditch somewhere has lifted the mood of the bridal party, but Chad and Brandy are still worried that she hasn't come home. As far as I'm concerned, she takes huffing to a whole other level and deserves a medal for her performance, but I can hardly voice my thoughts on the matter without sounding petty. At least she didn't succeed in totally spoiling our day.

"I tried texting Mom again," Brandy says to Chad. "I told her we were going to cut the cake soon and she was welcome to join us." She throws me a chagrined look. "Hope that's okay."

I shrug. "She was invited. It was her choice not to come."

"I know. Trust me, no one's blaming you, Eva," Brandy replies. "Anyway, she never responded to my text, so I doubt she'll show up for the cake either."

"Speaking of cake, it's that time," Martina says, as the DJ gets back on the microphone.

"Ladies and gentlemen," his voice booms out, "the bride and groom will now cut the cake."

"Do I look okay?" I ask Robin, patting some loose strands of hair as I get to my feet.

"Flawless. That make-up job is guaranteed to last well past midnight, Cinderella," she replies.

I take my place next to Chad and we smile endearingly at the photographer with the knife poised between us. I struggle to keep the smile fixed on my face as the memory of the bloody knife at my shower flashes to mind. Why would Laura do something despicable? And what did the message mean: *Beware the killer among you.* Did she mean me? I know she's been spreading rumors about me.

Does she really believe I would kill her? I toss my head, but I can't rid myself of the enticing thought. It would be one way to make sure she never comes between me and Chad again.

18

I let out a silent sigh of relief when our plane takes off from LAX, bound for Maui, the following afternoon. I scrutinized every passenger in the boarding area, and I'm certain Laura's not on the flight, which is a good start. Chad did his best to try and talk me into postponing our honeymoon, but I was adamant I was going with or without him. I'm not interested in hanging around waiting until his mother decides to show up before continuing on with the rest of my life. As far as I'm concerned, she's exhibiting the equivalent behavior of a toddler throwing a temper tantrum. By missing our wedding entirely, she left everyone on tenterhooks—an audacious way to express her disapproval of our union. I have no intention of playing along with her games.

Unable to check in with his sister for the next six hours, Chad plugs in his earphones and starts watching an action movie. I snuggle up next to him and select the same one on my screen. It's not my preferred genre, but at least we'll have something to talk about later. I feel as though his mother has dominated every conversation we've had in the past couple of days.

After the movie ends, Chad promptly falls asleep. I try to curb my irritation, knowing he didn't sleep well worrying about his mother. I can't help resenting everything about that woman. She's either intruding in our lives, or hovering over them like a shadow, but she's never far away.

The minute we land in Maui, Chad calls Brandy to check in. His forehead creases in concentration as he listens to whatever information she's relaying to him. I can't glean much from his side of the conversation. "Yeah ... uh-huh ... okay ... I see ... keep me posted."

I raise a questioning brow when he hangs up.

"Brandy doesn't know where she's gone," he says, sounding disheartened.

"Has she been over to your mom's house to check if there's any clues as to where she went?" I ask.

Chad nods, a stricken expression on his face. "Yes. Her wedding outfit is gone. It seems as though she was planning on attending. Something must have changed her mind."

I bite my tongue. She might have wanted to give the impression that she was going to the wedding, but, as wily and underhanded as she is, it means nothing.

"I feel kind of bad that we're here," Chad says, as we walk down to baggage claim together.

"Why? It's our honeymoon," I say, trying not to sound petulant. "There's nothing you can do in LA. anyway. Brandy's there whenever your mother decides to show back up. Sitting in your house fretting isn't going to accomplish anything."

"You're right. It's just that we're so far away if we do need to hurry back for any reason." He reaches for my hand. "I know the past couple of days have been difficult for you. I want our honeymoon to be perfect, but these are unusual circumstances. You're going to have to show me some grace. I know you don't get along with my mother, but I can't ignore the fact that she still hasn't come home."

"I get it," I say. "I understand you're going to be checking in with Brandy, but let's not make your mother the focus of every minute of every day."

"Deal," he says, grinning at me.

We retrieve our bags and make our way to the rental car booth to pick up our vehicle.

After stopping to purchase a few groceries, Chad punches the address of our Airbnb into the GPS and we settle in for the thirty-minute drive to the oceanfront North Shore beach house we've booked for our stay.

The closer we get, the more terrified I become of who might be waiting there to greet us.

19

Thankfully, my paranoid fears that my mother-in-law is planning to crash our honeymoon never materialize. Instead, we find a gift basket filled with fruit, chocolates, and a bottle of champagne on the kitchen counter to welcome us.

Chad wheels our suitcases into the master bedroom, then returns to admire the oceanfront view from the main living area.

"Stunning, isn't it?" I say, popping a grape into my mouth. "I wonder if the welcome gift is from the owners of the Airbnb, or one of our bridal party?"

"Let's find out." Chad reaches for a small envelope I failed to notice tucked under the fruit bowl and tears it open. His expression darkens.

"What is it?" I ask.

"Nothing," he says, hastily stuffing the card back into the envelope.

"It's not nothing if you don't want to show it to me," I say, snatching the envelope out of his hand. I slide the card out and read it: *beware the killer among you.*

I clap a hand to my mouth, my heart thundering in my chest. "This is from your mother," I say, my voice quivering.

Chad throws his hands up in the air. "Why do you immediately blame her for everything? You have absolutely no proof."

"It's the same message I got at my bridal shower. She tried to derail it, and when that didn't work, she wandered off and pretended she'd passed out. She's a sick, scary woman, and I hope I never set eyes on her again."

"She's the one who's afraid of you," Chad throws back at me. "She thought you planted the knife at the shower and wrote the note to scare her."

"That's rich," I scoff. "Do you think I left myself a note on my honeymoon too? If your mother was afraid of me, she wouldn't spend every minute of every day insulting me and running me down to everyone within earshot."

"While you tell everyone how much you'd like to ring her neck," Chad retorts. "She's not the one with the explosive temper."

"What's that supposed to mean?"

"You dumped a water bottle over her head and stormed off afterward."

"Only because she ruined our rehearsal on purpose."

"She passed out, Eva. Show some pity, for goodness sake."

I curl my hand into a fist, seething inwardly. "Pity is wasted on vindictive people. Someone needs to call her out on her atrocious behavior."

"She's lonely and she misses Shana."

I let out a disgusted snort. "So now we're bringing your deceased wife on our honeymoon, as well as your mother. I'm out." I snatch the bottle of champagne from the counter and stomp out of the room.

Ensconced in the master bathroom, I fill the Jacuzzi tub and pop the cork on the champagne. This isn't at all how I envisioned spending my honeymoon, alone in a bubble bath, swigging champagne from a bottle.

"Congratulations, Laura," I say to the mirror. "You managed to hitch a ride here after all."

20

I wake the following morning to the smell of freshly-brewed coffee. I swing my legs over the edge of the bed and stretch, taking in the stunning ocean view beyond our window. Today's the first full day of our honeymoon and I'm determined to make sure it's a memorable one. Chad apologized profusely to me last night for his baseless accusation—admitting that he was tired and stressed out between the wedding and his mother going missing, and he lost it. In the end we agreed to put the whole fiasco behind us until we get back to LA, and focus on enjoying our time together in Maui.

"How about we take a helicopter ride?" Chad suggests, when I join him in the kitchen where he's browsing websites of things to do. "It says here we get to see hidden waterfalls inaccessible by land, and they fly us over the ridgelines of the rugged West Maui mountains and the rainforest. The whole trip is narrated, which should be interesting."

"That all sounds good, but is it safe?" I ask, pouring myself a coffee.

"It must be—they're taking tourists up every day," Chad

replies. "If they weren't bringing them back safely, they'd be out of business. Anyway, driving is way more dangerous than air travel."

"I know they say that, but I always feel safer when I'm on the ground."

Chad curls an arm around my waist and pulls me in for a kiss. "You said you wanted to make some special memories. This is your chance. Try something different. Walk on the wild side for a change."

I'm still a little skittish about the whole idea, but he manages to talk me into it. "Okay, I'll go on the condition you go snorkeling with me afterward."

"Awesome! Let me make a couple of calls and see if I can book us a tour today."

I set about whipping up some omelettes for breakfast while Chad haggles with the tour companies.

"Good news," he says, when he hangs up. "We've got a spot later this morning."

"That's great," I say, trying to sound enthusiastic as I serve up our omelettes. We sit down together to eat, and Chad pulls up the trailer video from the helicopter company.

"Before we watch that, I think we should talk about this again," I say, pointing to the card still lying in the gift basket where I tossed it. "I know you don't want to believe your mother is capable of doing something like this, but she already tried to ruin my bridal shower, and our wedding—why not the honeymoon too?"

Chad drags a hand through his tousled hair. "How would she know where to have the gift basket delivered?"

"She has a key to your house. She might have seen your email confirmation from the Airbnb."

"I know she's a pain at times, but I just can't see her

sending that sick note. It could have been anyone in the bridal party—they might have seen the address when they were at your place."

"Like who? My sister, your sister? That makes no sense."

Chad frowns. "What about that childhood friend of yours, Cindi—the one you haven't seen in decades?"

"Why would she try and sabotage my wedding? She was my best friend in school."

"People change, Eva. You don't know her anymore."

I roll my eyes. "Maybe you don't know your mother as well as you think you do either."

The trill of Chad's phone interrupts us. "It's Brandy. I'd better take this." He hits the speaker button and places the phone on the table in front of him.

I stab at my omelette as I listen in.

"Chad!" Brandy says, her voice trembling with emotion. "Mom finally called me back."

"Thank goodness!" Chad scrunches his eyes shut and lets out a relieved breath. "What did she have to say for herself?"

"She's demanding that Eva apologize in person for humiliating her at the rehearsal."

Chad's eyes lock with mine. "And if she doesn't?"

There's a long pause before Brandy replies, "She's threatening to kill herself."

21

My jaw drops at Brandy's words. I throw Chad an indignant look, hoping he'll speak up in my defense, but instead he stares morosely down at his phone. I'm in a no-win position—under pressure to apologize to the very person I swore off all contact with. She's the one who should be apologizing to me. She tried to humiliate me by throwing red wine all over my dress at my bridal shower. This latest demand is just another example of my mother-in-law's despicable attempts to sabotage my relationship with Chad. If I agree to apologize, she'll take a victory lap and use it as proof that I'm at fault. But if I refuse, I'll be held responsible for any pathetic attempt she makes to swallow a handful of sleeping pills or whatever other scheme she's working on. She has no intention of killing herself, but she wouldn't hesitate to stage a suicide attempt if it made me look bad. And people will blame me. I've lost count of how many times I've wished her dead in the earshot of others.

"If I agree to apologize to her," I say through gritted teeth. "It's only fair to expect her to reciprocate."

"Eva, please—" Chad begins, but I hold up my hand to cut him off.

"I warned you I wasn't going to let her trample all over me any more, and I'm not going to back off now, no matter what she threatens to do."

Brandy clears her throat. "Why don't you two discuss it and call me back when you've reached a decision."

She hangs up and I glare across the table at Chad. "Thanks for nothing. You should have spoken up in my defense. You know how atrociously your mother treats me, and I put up with it, for your sake. She couldn't even be bothered to show up to our wedding after trying to sabotage it. I'm done with her."

Chad rubs a hand wearily over his brow. "I know, and I'm sorry. It's just that Brandy sounded like she was at a breaking point. I was hoping you would agree to apologize so we can end this standoff, if nothing else. You're right that Mom needs to apologize to you, too. But someone has to go first."

I stare out at the ocean for a long moment, at war with my own emotions. I hate how much this is hurting Chad. If an apology is what it takes to pacify everyone, then I'll do it, but that's the last contact I'll ever have with Laura Turner. I never want to see her sour face again after this.

"Fine. I'll be the bigger person," I say, "so long as you and Brandy make it clear to your mother that I expect her to reciprocate." I drain my mug of coffee and check the time. "We need to get dressed if we're going to make our tour."

Chad stares at me horrorstruck. "What are you talking about? We can't go ahead with it now. We need to call the airline and change our tickets."

I let out an aggrieved gasp. "You've got to be kidding me! We're not cutting short our honeymoon to accommodate your mother's latest antics. I'll apologize to her once we get home."

"Eva, she's threatening to commit suicide. She's not thinking straight. We can't wait until we've perfected our suntans before we address the situation."

"Give me a break! She's not going to kill herself! I guarantee this is just another cry for attention to derail our honeymoon. You talked me into this helicopter ride, and we can't get a refund last minute, so I'm going, with or without you." I get to my feet with a loud screech of my chair. "I'm going to get changed. You decide if you want to come with me, or fly home without me."

"Wait! Can't we compromise?" Chad says. "How about we stay here today, and fly home tomorrow. I'll make it up to you, I promise. We can come back to Maui another time and stay as long as you want."

I shake my head in disgust. "Do you really think I'd want to come back here with all the bad memories I'm going to associate with this place now? Your mother has ruined Maui for me, just like she's ruined everything else. But I can tell you this, I'm not going to let her ruin the rest of my life."

"If she follows through on her threat, I'll never forgive myself for putting a helicopter ride ahead of her wellbeing," Chad says.

"Your choice," I say with a shrug.

I stash my mug in the sink and stomp out of the kitchen, shaking with indignation. I know how this is going to end. It's a losing proposition for me. If I don't agree to cut short our honeymoon, and Laura harms herself, Chad and Brandy will hold it against me forever, and my marriage won't survive the fallout.

And if I let Chad fly back without me, Laura will have succeeded in separating us. I can't let that happen.

22

Strapped in our seats in the helicopter with our headphones on, I'm enthralled by the narrated trip over the stunning mountains and waterfalls of Maui. Up here, I can almost forget about the nightmare that awaits me on the ground. Chad's feigning enjoyment of the trip, but he's secretly checking his phone every few minutes, as though terrified of receiving bad news. Despite my reluctance, I've agreed to his compromise proposal to spend the day here and fly back to LA tomorrow. I'm not sure what he said to Brandy when he called her back, but she's bound to be relieved that we're coming home. I respect her for not pressuring us, and letting us come to the decision on our own. She knows how difficult her mother can be, and she's seen firsthand how badly she treats me. She's got to know what a huge sacrifice this is on my part after everything I endured leading up to the wedding.

Exhilarated and hungry after our helicopter ride, we find a local fish market to eat lunch at. We take a seat at a communal table with our Mahi-Mahi fish and chips, and settle in to enjoy the music playing in the background.

"This coleslaw's incredible," I say, loading another mouthful on my fork. "It doesn't get much fresher than this."

"Hmm," Chad replies, his eyes glued to his phone.

"Can't you put that thing away for a few minutes? We've already reduced our honeymoon to one day, so how about you spend it with me instead of on your phone worrying about your mother and her latest histrionics?"

"I wasn't worrying about her. I was worrying about you," he replies. "I was just thinking during that helicopter ride that we should take out life insurance policies when we get back home. I don't want you to have to worry about anything, if something should happen to me."

I stop chewing and frown. "That's kind of morbid. Do we have to discuss this right now?"

Chad gives a chagrined shrug. "No, of course not." He reaches for my hand and kisses me gently on the knuckles. "I just don't want to lose you, Eva. I can't go through that again."

I flinch at the oblique reference to Shana. It stings to know he was thinking about his first wife on our honeymoon, but I know it was only because he wants to protect me.

"Thank you for the sacrifice you're making," he goes on. "I know how much you've been looking forward to this honeymoon to recover from all the stress of the wedding, and now it's ruined too. But I promise you, I'm going to spend the rest of my life making it up to you."

"I second that idea," I say with a mischievous wink, in a bid to lighten the mood. Death, life insurance, mothers-in-law, and first wives should all be banned topics on a honeymoon in my book.

After some good food and music, my mood lifts, and we

spend the rest of the afternoon snorkeling and lazing around on the beach in what turns out to be a perfect day. But as the sun begins to set, dread fills my heart.

I've obligated myself to returning to face my enemy and grovel for forgiveness. I don't want her forgiveness. I want her eliminated from my life.

23

B randy picks us up from LAX airport the following afternoon. We load our bags, packed with clean clothes and unused sunscreen, into her Lexus and climb aboard.

"You look like you got some sun for the short time you were there," she says.

"We spent yesterday afternoon on the beach," I say, stifling a yawn. "Is your mother expecting us to go over there this evening, or can this apology wait until the morning?"

Brandy flinches. "I don't think it will happen this evening. She hasn't come home yet, and she still won't tell me where she is."

"Are you serious?" Chad says. "So, technically she's still AWOL. Why didn't you tell me that?"

Brandy shrugs. "I didn't want to worry you any more then you already were."

"I'd rather not be kept in the dark," Chad complains.

"I'm sure she'll come back now that she's achieved her mission to ruin our honeymoon," I say, the words flying from my lips before I can rein them in.

Brandy shoots me a sympathetic glance in the rearview mirror, but Chad stares straight ahead, face like thunder. He's mad at all three women in his life right now—me for my sarcastic take on things, Brandy for not letting him know the full extent of the situation, and his mother for putting us through this torture to begin with.

"I'll text Mom once I drop you two off and let her know you're home," Brandy says. "I'm sure it will be tomorrow at this point before she agrees to meet."

I snap my lips into a tight line. No doubt, she's relishing the idea of hearing me apologize to her in person. But it won't be an apology without strings. There's a long list of things I intend to tell her in return.

After Brandy drops us off at our house, it doesn't take me long to fall into a deep sleep. I wake the following morning, completely disoriented in my new surroundings. Chad's side of the bed is cold. I get to my feet and pad downstairs to brew some coffee. I'll have to suffer through drinking it black as we have no creamer in the house. There's no sign of Chad anywhere. I hope he hasn't gone to meet his mother without me. We need to put up a united front.

I slump down in a kitchen chair to sip my coffee and scroll through my phone browsing furniture stores. I can't wait for our new house to be finished. Living in the home Shana shared with Chad is not ideal—her stamp is on everything.

I'm shopping couches when Chad comes barreling through the back door.

"I was wondering where you went," I say.

"Just adjusting the sprinklers. The grass is turning brown."

I glance out the window at our sorry-looking lawn. Shana was an avid gardener—as I've been reminded on multiple occasions—but neither Chad nor I have much of a green thumb. "So, what's the plan? Have you heard from your mother?"

He shakes his head. "Brandy said she'll text me as soon as she hears something. She let Mom know last night that we were back in town and wanted to get together."

"Get together, is that what we're calling it now? It does sound friendlier than a summons," I say, with a bitter edge.

Chad wisely ignores the comment as he pours himself a coffee.

"There's nothing in the house to eat," I say. "Do you want to go grab some breakfast?"

"Sure. We might as well swing by the apartment while we're out and pick up the rest of your stuff now that we're home."

"I'll ask Robin if she wants to join us." I say, tapping out a quick message to her.

She responds with a thumbs up and we arrange to meet at The Lucky Hen Café, just around the corner from the apartment.

I get dressed and apply minimal make up. If this meeting with Laura goes ahead this morning, I don't want to look like I tried too hard, but I don't want to look like a total grunge either. It will only be fodder for her to use against me in another one of her diatribes.

"Still nothing from your mother?" I ask Chad when we sit down at our table in the restaurant.

He gives a frustrated shake of his head.

Before we can discuss the situation any further, Robin arrives. "So, how was your *very* short honeymoon?" she asks with a wry grin as she pulls out a chair.

I grimace. "That wasn't the only issue. When we arrived

at the Airbnb, there was a gift basket on the counter with a nasty note to greet us."

I register the shock on Robin's face.

"What did it say?" she asks, reaching for the glass of water in front of her.

"The same thing as the card at the shower: *Beware the killer among you.*"

Robin's face pales. "But that means whoever is behind it knew the address of where you were staying."

"Exactly," I say, arching a brow. "And guess who has a key to Chad's house."

24

I t's been three days since we arrived back from our very brief honeymoon in Maui. Laura still hasn't contacted Brandy to arrange our meeting—or summons, as I'm calling it due to Laura's terms and conditions. I know she's only dragging this out so she can make the early days of my marriage as miserable as possible, but Chad's working himself up into a frenzy again, worrying that something has happened to her—I can't deny I wish that were the case.

I've made the most of my time off work by moving the rest of my stuff out of Robin's apartment and into Chad's place. Now that I'm finished unpacking, there doesn't seem to be much point in hanging around the house any longer. I'd rather be back at work where I can focus on something other than my psycho mother-in-law. I make a call to my boss, Poppy, who's only too delighted to have me come back as soon as possible.

Chad's far from happy when I break the news to him. "We could have spent the time doing something together. I can't go back to work until next week—I've already got someone covering my shift at the hospital."

I squeeze my head in my hands. "I'm not going to sit in the house twiddling my thumbs waiting on your mother to decide she's made us sweat long enough."

"And what if that's not the case?" Chad asks."What if something really has happened to her this time?"

I roll my eyes. "If you're so worried about her, call the police."

"Brandy tried that already. They're not going to do anything. They think it's a domestic issue, based on the texts Brandy and Mom have exchanged."

"Well, they're not wrong. That's exactly what it is," I say, getting to my feet. "I'm going to iron my clothes. I promised Poppy I'd be back at my desk tomorrow. If your mother wants to meet me, it's going to have to be after work hours. I'm not taking any more time off to accommodate her whims."

When I walk into the office the following morning, my colleagues greet me with uncertain smiles and furtive glances. I'm not sure how much Poppy has told them, or what they've gleaned from the rumor mill, but the very fact that I'm home from my honeymoon early signals something is amiss.

I've barely set my purse down, before Poppy calls me into her office. "I'm sorry you had to cut your honeymoon short, Eva. I'm not going to pry into the details, but I just wanted to say I hope your mother-in-law's all right."

I twist my lips. "I wish I felt that much goodwill toward her," I say. "She's done everything possible to ruin my wedding and honeymoon. I'm not exactly feeling warm and fuzzy about her at the moment."

Poppy rests her elbows on the desk and tents her fingers

in front of her. "In-laws can be difficult. If there's anything I can do to help, or if you need to take any more time off, please let me know."

"Thanks. I appreciate that, but I'm happy to be back at work. I need something else to focus on."

"Well, there's no shortage of work. It's been stacking up on your desk."

I get to my feet. "In that case, I'd better go make a dent in it."

Poppy raises a hand to halt me. "Before I forget, a courier delivered this for you yesterday. I had to sign for it."

I take the expensive-looking oversized cream envelope from her and stare at it, frowning. My pulse begins to throb in my temples. It's from the law offices of Sterling and Hackett. *Laura's lawyer is Roger Hackett.* My thoughts take a deep dive. Could this be something to do with the water bottle incident? Surely my mother-in-law isn't planning on suing me for assault.

25

I take the envelope back to my desk and stuff it into my purse. I can't read it now under the watchful eyes of my colleagues. No wonder Laura's been dragging her heels about meeting up with me. She's decided to go one step further and pursue legal recourse—or threaten to at least. Why else would the letter have been delivered by courier and require a signature? Does dumping a bottle of water over someone's head really count as assault? I might be in a whole lot more trouble than I anticipated. After all, she had the entire bridal party as witnesses to the incident, including the minister. It's not as if I can deny what I did. I'm not even sorry. I'd do it again in a heartbeat.

I power up my computer and start cleaning out my inbox, tackling the most important emails and deleting anything irrelevant. My eyes keep wandering to my purse. I feel as though the envelope is burning a hole through the leather. But I don't want to read it in front of my colleagues —I might not be able to keep my emotions in check. Rose, the other legal intern and resident gossip guru, is typing away on her keyboard only a few feet from me. As eagle-eyed as she is, she'd notice if I pulled the envelope out, and know by my reaction on reading it that something was wrong. I don't want to talk about it with anyone before I've even had a chance to process it myself.

I force myself to focus on my screen, reading and rereading the words floating in and out of my vision, but it's no use. I can't think about anything other than that wretched envelope. I throw a sidelong glance at Rose, then reach for my purse and get up from my desk.

"Too much coffee this morning. It's running straight through me," I quip as I walk past her.

She smiles hesitantly, curiosity flickering over her face, and I immediately regret over-explaining the fact that I'm headed to the bathroom. It sounds like I'm hiding something, even to my own ears.

Locked inside a stall, I hang my purse up on the back of the door and unzip it.

Just as I reach for the envelope, I hear a voice call out, "Everything okay, Eva?"

I scrunch my eyes shut and groan inwardly. Rose has picked up on my unease. I know she's only being compassionate, given everything that's happened, but right now I just need a few minutes to myself.

"Fine, thanks." I clench my jaw, hoping to hear the sound of the door closing as she heads back to her desk, but apparently she's planning on waiting for me.

"I'm worried about you," she says. "I still can't believe you cut your honeymoon short because of your mother-in-law. I know you two don't have that great of a relationship to begin with. Is she sick or something? I heard she couldn't make the wedding."

Sick in the head. I curl my fingers into a fist. "Yeah, something like that. She's been experiencing symptoms. Chad was really worried about her, so he talked me into coming home early."

I flush the toilet and walk out of the cubicle. The envelope will have to wait for a more opportune time.

Rose folds her arms and leans back against the sink, observing me. "You're going to have to take a stand, you know. You can't let your mother-in-law dictate the rest of your life just because you're married to her son."

I frown as I think about the envelope—almost certainly containing bad news. So far, Laura has done a pretty good job of dictating how things are going. I'm beginning to feel like a puppet on a string, and that doesn't sit well with me. Chad's not wrong about my explosive temper.

My mother-in-law's lucky I didn't douse her in gasoline instead of water.

26

I don't get the chance to open the envelope at lunchtime either because Rose insists on taking me out to eat to "cheer me up," as she puts it. I pick at my chicken sandwich and try to concentrate as she rattles on about everything that happened in the office during my absence.

"Are you even listening to a word I said?" Rose asks.

"I'm sorry," I say shaking my head. "I zoned out for a minute. I probably shouldn't have come back to work today. I'm exhausted—emotionally and physically. Chad's so worried about his mom that he's barely sleeping, and he keeps me awake because he's so restless."

Rose cocks her head to one side. "At the risk of being nosy, what are her symptoms exactly, other than a general case of nastiness and frequent bouts of vitriol?"

I venture a guarded smile. I'm not about to tell anyone at work about my mother-in-law's standoff—not until I know what that envelope contains. "You've pretty much nailed it, at least when it comes to me. The weird thing is that she loved Chad's first wife, Shana. She never misses an opportunity to tell me how wonderful she was."

Rose stirs the ice cubes at the bottom of her glass with her straw, looking contemplative. "Do you think she's just saying that to upset you?"

"I don't think so. Chad said they were really close."

Rose holds my gaze. "Do you believe him?"

"Of course. Why would he lie to me?"

Rose shrugs, looking uncomfortable. "So that you would marry him. It would have scared you off if he'd told you what a mean-spirited mother-in-law Laura was to Shana."

I shake my head. "No. Even Brandy says her mom was very fond of Shana. Whatever Laura's beef is, it's with me. Although, she's upset with Chad at the moment too. She won't even text him back."

"Why not?"

I scrunch my eyes shut, debating how much to disclose. I shouldn't really tell Rose what's going on because she won't be able to keep it to herself, but I need to get it off my chest. "Okay, here's the thing. I did something stupid. I got mad at Laura for interrupting the rehearsal with her fainting fit, or whatever it was. She was making a huge fuss and getting all the attention. She asked for water so I grabbed a bottle from a pew nearby and poured it over her."

Rose bursts out laughing and claps a hand to her mouth. "She totally deserved a cold shower. I can't believe you invited her to the wedding after that."

"She didn't show up. We were on tenterhooks the entire time, afraid she would burst through the church door and object, or make a dramatic entrance at the reception and cause a scene, so my wedding day ended up being all about Laura Turner anyway."

"You have to put your foot down," Rose says. "If I were

you, I'd tell Chad he needs to choose between you or his mother."

I let out a heavy sigh. "I did, but she took it to the next level and did a disappearing act. No one's seen her since the rehearsal. She's not at her house and she'll only communicate with Chad and Brandy by text."

Rose's eyes grow wide. "Sounds like the perfect solution to me."

"She says she's not going to come back until I apologize to her. She's claiming I assaulted her by dumping water on her. She even threatened to commit suicide, which is baloney, but that's why we came back early from Maui."

Rose shakes her head in disbelief. "Unbelievable! Don't apologize, and you won't have to ever see her again. Either she disappears for good, or she knocks herself off. Problem solved."

I grimace. "I don't think my husband would ever forgive me if anything were to happen to her. Anyway, I agreed to apologize under the condition she apologizes to me too. We were supposed to meet days ago, but she keeps dragging things out and leaving us hanging. It's been three days since she last texted Brandy."

"She's holding you all hostage; that's what she's doing," Rose says.

I press my lips into a tight line. She's right. I'm letting Laura do exactly what I said I wouldn't. I need to put an end to this before my mother-in-law destroys the rest of my life too.

27

The afternoon flies by as I work methodically through the backlog of cases that have accumulated in the few days I've been gone. When five o'clock rolls around, I waste no time packing my bag and making a hasty exit before Rose can waylay me and talk me into going for a drink. I don't want company right now. I'm going to find a quiet coffee shop somewhere off the beaten track where I can open the correspondence from Laura's attorney and read it in peace, and take whatever amount of time I need to think about what my response is going to be —short of putting her in a body bag.

I'm beginning to rethink the wisdom of allowing Chad to continue to pursue any kind of relationship with his mother. If she's determined to keep harassing me, then my husband needs to make a clean break with her too. He can't reward her for bad behavior, and if she's suing me, she might as well be suing him as well. If it comes to choosing between the two of us, Chad has to side with me or our marriage is over, effective immediately.

I exit the building and hurry across the parking lot to my

car. After driving around for a bit, I find a small, nondescript coffee shop on a side street that's perfect for my purpose. Inside, I'm relieved to see only two other customers—both buried in their phones. I order a decaf latte and carry it to one of the empty tables.

I wait until the employee who's busy wiping down tables goes back behind the counter, before unzipping my purse and pulling out the envelope. I throw a furtive glance around, but no one is paying me the slightest bit of attention.

Just as I'm about to open the envelope, an elderly woman waddles through the door and makes her way up to the counter. After placing her order, she turns around to scope out a table. I drop my gaze, not wanting to relay any sense of camaraderie. The last thing I need right now is to be forced to engage in conversation with a lonely looking, elderly stranger.

I watch from behind my shield of hair as she picks up her order and carries it across the café. She sets it on a table, then changes her mind, and picks it up again. I grimace when she begins walking in my direction. Reaching for my phone, I make a point of keeping my attention fixed on the screen, all the while surreptitiously observing the woman as she pulls out a chair at the table next to mine. I sense her eyes on me, but I continue scrolling through my apps.

After a few minutes, I chance a glance in the woman's direction. To my relief, she's sipping her coffee and studying her own phone. I let out a slow, silent breath, then tear open the envelope and pull out a folded page, along with a smaller envelope. My eyes dart across the page, shock rendering the words incomprehensible.

"Bad news dear?"

I almost jump out of my seat at the unfamiliar voice. The

woman at the next table is looking straight at me, head cocked to one side, her wrinkles molded into an expression of concern.

I give a nonchalant shake of my head, despite the fact that my insides are churning. "No. Just work stuff."

She tinkles a laugh. "I must admit it's such a relief to be retired. I don't miss the stress of those days. What kind of work do you do?" She gestures to the envelope on the table. "Are you an attorney?"

I gather my things and jump to my feet. "Excuse me. I just realized the time. I need to get going."

I scurry out of the coffee shop and back to my car. Safely inside, I slide down in the seat and scrunch my eyes shut, trying to stop myself from shaking. When my heartbeat begins to slow, I pull the envelope back out of my purse and reread the cover page.

DEAR MRS. EVA TURNER,

I was instructed by my client, Laura Turner, to forward the enclosed letter to you, in the event she failed to check in with my office, as she has been doing on a monthly basis for the past two years. I am merely the intermediary and not privy to the contents of this letter.

Sincerely,
Roger Hackett

FROWNING, I tear open the smaller envelope and pull out the letter in question.

As I begin to read, a tsunami of anger rises up inside me. So this is her next ploy to destroy my marriage. It will never work. I won't get suckered into her lies.

28

Dear Eva,

If you're reading this, I'm dead, and my son killed me. He also killed his first wife. I know you think I hate you, but nothing could be further from the truth. I am your ally, and my only goal is to protect you. While it's true that everything I did was designed to drive you away, it wasn't for the reasons you think. I realize this is going to come as a huge shock to you, but I'm asking you to read this letter through with an open mind.

I loved Shana from the first moment I met her. She was everything I could have wished for in a daughter-in-law, and I reminded Chad constantly how lucky he was to have her in his life. They seemed genuinely happy together, and neither Brandy nor I ever witnessed anything to the contrary. We were all devastated at Shana's untimely death. At least I thought we were, until I found out that Chad killed her.

I'm sure you're wondering how I came to this horrific conclusion. The first red flag was when I found out that Shana and Chad had taken out five-million-dollar life insurance policies on each other. It seemed like an exorbitant amount for a nurse and a fitness instructor. But my misgivings were not just because of the large insurance policy Chad inherited after Shana's death, or even the freak accident. There's more to it than that. Please keep reading, and don't shred this letter when you're done. You're going to need it as evidence.

Several weeks after Shana's death, I was in Chad's house looking for photos to make a special album to commemorate her. To my horror, I discovered her wedding ring, engagement ring, and cross necklace in a box full of miscellaneous photos. What you need to understand is that she never took those pieces of jewelry off, but the police said she wasn't wearing any jewelry when she was found. Even now, I can still feel the sinking feeling in my bones when I set eyes on them. I went home and thought it over, not wanting to believe that my own son could be a killer.

After a sleepless night, I decided I had to share my suspicions with the police. But when I went back to look for the jewelry, it was gone. Without evidence, the police were unwilling to investigate. They had already talked to Chad at the time of Shana's death, and he cooperated fully with them. Her death was declared an accident, and there was nothing in the autopsy to indicate otherwise—no drugs or sedatives in her system, no blunt force trauma, no signs of strangulation. Her injuries were consistent with a fall. What do I think? I believe she was pushed.

I understand you might be skeptical of what you're reading, especially after my failed attempts to scare you off, but my advice to you is "run." Ignore it at your own peril. We won't be able to have a conversation about this because I won't be coming back. Chad must have decided it was time to muzzle me. I don't know how, but my guess is that he found out somehow that I shared my suspicions with the police. Someone must have tipped him off. As a nurse, he has friends who are emergency responders and cops, so it's not beyond the realm of possibility. But this isn't about me any longer. You need to divorce him immediately and protect your assets.

You might be wondering why I never confronted Chad directly. I was tempted to, but I couldn't prove anything, and without the police on my side, I knew I would be putting myself in danger. I shared my suspicions with Brandy, but she didn't believe me either. She thinks my nerves were frayed after Shana's death. She idolizes her brother and remains convinced that his only thought was to protect Shana when he took out the life insurance policies. He has his sister fooled, just as he had me fooled for the longest time.

I need you to finish what I started. I need you to prove that Chad killed Shana. Search his phone, his computer, his closet—anywhere you think you might find evidence. I doubt they will ever find my body, but if they do, please have me cremated and my ashes scattered on the ocean, as stipulated in my will.

Sincerely,

Laura Turner

I SCRUNCH the letter up in my fist and hurl it over my shoulder into the back seat. That woman can really spin a story. If she thinks I'm going to buy this ridiculous tale and divorce her son, only for her to show up again in triumph, she's sorely mistaken. I'm not going to let her make me a laughing stock. It's truly unbelievable the lengths my mother-in-law will go to in her hate-filled campaign to get rid of me.

The bottom line is, she doesn't think I'm good enough for her son, and she never will. Shana may have been everything she wished for in a daughter-in-law, but I'm not.

I'm her worst nightmare. By the time I'm done with her, she's going to wish she were dead.

29

I barely sleep that night, the contents of Laura's letter going round and round like a wash cycle in my brain. When I stumble into the kitchen the following morning, Chad raises his brows at the sight of my tousled hair and rumpled sweats. "You look a little rough. Are you feeling okay?"

"I think I might be coming down with something," I say, averting my gaze.

"Just as well it's Saturday," he replies. "Why don't you go back to bed and I'll bring you a coffee?"

I walk over to the coffee machine and slip a pod in. "Thanks, but I don't think I'm going to be able to sleep now anyway."

Chad pushes his iPad to one side and curls his fingers around his oversized mug. "What do you fancy doing today? Want to catch a movie this afternoon?"

I frown, trying to drum up an excuse. I texted Robin a few minutes ago, but I haven't heard back from her yet. I need to get her take on this letter. I'm ninety-nine-percent convinced it's just Laura leveling up her nefarious game again, but that one percent is niggling at me. "Actually, I made plans to go shopping with Robin."

"Sure you're up for that?"

"I guess we'll find out," I say, sipping my coffee.

"In that case, I might see if I can talk Jim into a round of golf," Chad says.

I give an approving nod. "Good idea. I'll be gone most of the day anyway." I'm still debating whether or not to tell Chad about the letter. I would have done it last night, but I want to hear Robin's opinion first, before I do something I might regret.

After showering and getting dressed, I feel marginally better. Robin confirmed that she's free so I suggested meeting at the mall. Shopping is the last thing on my mind this morning, but it's a small price to pay to get my sister's opinion on Laura's wild claims.

"I'm glad you called," she says, walking up to me at the main entrance to the mall. "I've been meaning to look for some new workout gear. My leggings are stretched so thin, they're almost see-through at this point. Not a good look."

"Lead the way," I say, striking an upbeat tone.

I try to focus as she drags me in and out of fitness clothing stores, but I can't bring myself to try anything on.

"Which leggings do you like best?" she asks, sticking her head out of yet another dressing room. "I'm wavering between the two colors."

"Me too," I say plastering a grin on my face. I have no idea which colors she's wavering between because I've been too preoccupied with my thoughts about the letter.

She eventually settles on some espresso-colored leggings and carries them up to the cashier.

"Ready for a break?" I ask, as we walk out of the store.

She laughs. "Where's your stamina? Don't you remember the days when we shopped 'till we dropped?"

I give her a wry grin. "Vaguely. That was back when we were teenagers."

"Fair enough. There's a Starbucks at the top of the escalator."

We manage to snag a table and Robin holds it while I fetch our drinks.

"I need to talk to you about something," I say, setting down our cappuccinos.

She raises her brows. "I had a feeling you were brooding about something. Is it Laura?"

I give a glum nod.

She sighs. "Let me guess. She's increasing her demands before she agrees to accept your apology. Maybe she wants you to bow down in her presence, or better still, shuffle forward on your knees. Or maybe—"

"She's pretending to be dead."

Robin's jaw drops open. She stares at me aghast, clutching her cappuccino in a death grip. "What? I mean ... how?"

I reach into my purse and retrieve the envelope. "This was delivered to the office by courier. Poppy signed for it. It's from Laura, via her lawyer."

Robin reaches out a tentative hand. "I'm guessing you want me to read it?"

"I need your opinion on it," I say, passing it to her. "I'm ninety-nine percent sure it's a complete scam, but—"

"But you think there's a possibility she's dead?" Robin cuts in.

Several women at the next table turn their heads in our direction.

"Yes, her dog's dead," I say loudly. "But she was fourteen so she lived a long and happy life."

The women's curious expressions dissolve into disinterest as they resume their conversation.

I lean across the table toward Robin.

"If what's in this letter is true, my life's in danger."

30

Robin looks visibly disturbed as she pulls out the letter. "Is she threatening to kill you or something? I don't understand. I thought you said she was pretending to be dead."

"She is. It's complicated. Just read the letter."

I wrap my hands around my coffee cup and study Robin's face as she begins to read. Her face knots in anxiety. From time to time, she glances up at me, a deep frown creasing her forehead. When she's done, she leans back in her chair without saying anything.

"What do you think?" I prod.

"She's seriously disturbed," Robin says.

I nod, feeling a measure of relief at my sister's diagnosis. The letter is nothing more than Laura ratcheting up her manipulation.

"I think you need to involve the police," Robin goes on. "If this doesn't work to drive you away, she might try to kill you next." Her eyes grow wide and she leans in closer. "What if *she* killed Shana?"

I rumple my brow. "Why would she do that? She adored her."

Robin arches a reproachful brow. "So she said. But she says a lot of things that aren't true. It's kind of odd that she mentioned believing that Shana was pushed."

I sip my cappuccino, considering this. Robin's not wrong. Laura could have had everyone fooled. Maybe she even talked Chad into taking out the life insurance policies so he would be financially solvent. I need to talk to him about that when I get home. I don't know too much about his financial situation before he cashed in on the life insurance policy. From what he told me, he used the money to pay off his debts, including his mortgage and Laura's, and buy a couple of rental properties.

I trace my finger around the lid of my cup. "I think you're right that the letter is just another attempt to break up my marriage, but I haven't shown it to Chad yet."

"Why not?" Robin asks, her tone sharpening. "He needs to know how despicable his mother really is."

I twist the ends of my hair around my finger. "There's one thing that's bugging me. When we were in Maui, Chad suggested we take out life insurance policies."

Robin doesn't respond right away, but I see fear in the tight line of her lips. "That is odd timing," she ventures. "Do you think Laura might have put the idea in his head?"

"I don't know. I was nervous about the helicopter ride, and Chad kept trying to reassure me that it was safe. That's what triggered the conversation about life insurance. It could have been a totally innocent coincidence."

"Maybe," Robin replies dubiously. "The alternative doesn't bear thinking about. What if Laura's telling the truth?"

I let out a snort. "That would be a first."

Robin wraps her fingers around her mug. "Do you think there's any chance she could be dead?"

I give a small shrug. "I think she's faking it. She's been psycho for as long as I've known her."

Robin wags a finger at me. "That's a good point. You haven't known her all that long. Maybe you should talk to someone who did, ask them if she's mentally unstable."

"You mean like her lawyer?"

"Possibly. Or Brandy. Speaking of which, are you going to tell her about the letter?"

"I don't think so, not yet, at any rate. It would devastate her to know her mother was making such vile accusations about her brother. I doubt she told Brandy anything. If she had, Brandy would have warned me."

"Just playing devil's advocate for a minute—what if those accusations turn out to be true?" Robin's gaze locks with mine, and I see terror glimmering in her eyes. "I don't want you to have an untimely accident like Shana."

31

I drop my head into my hands and drag my fingers through my hair. "I don't know what to do, Robin. I don't believe Chad had anything to do with Shana's death, but Laura has succeeded in making me doubt that our marriage can survive her wrecking campaign. She even asked me to finish what she started and prove that Chad killed Shana. How sick is that?"

Robin sips her cappuccino thoughtfully. "Maybe you should put him to the test."

"What do you mean?"

"Tell him you've changed your mind about taking out life insurance. See how he reacts. If he's not bothered, then you have nothing to worry about. On the other hand, if he kicks up a fuss about it, you might want to consider moving back in with me."

I throw her a startled look. "I'm not going to do that. That's exactly what Laura wants. I can't let her win. Just because Chad wants us to take out life insurance, it doesn't mean he killed his first wife, or that he's planning to kill me."

"Maybe not, but if I were you I might just pass on the life insurance for now. Are you going to show that letter to Chad?"

"I'm not sure. He'd be gutted by the kinds of things his mother is saying about him in the letter. Personally, I don't believe a word of it. Nothing in the letter makes sense. If Laura found Shana's jewelry in the house, why didn't she take a photo of it? My guess is that the police gave the jewelry back to Chad after they found Shana's body."

Robin chews her lip. "Ask him—see what he has to say about it. It might clear some things up."

"I don't know. If the letter's any indication of Laura's current state of mind, she's headed for involuntary psychiatric commitment."

Robin lets out a humph. "Maybe that's what needs to happen. Anyone who causes as much drama as she does needs professional help."

"You've got that right." I drain my coffee cup and slide my chair out. "I have to stretch my legs. Want to walk around the mall some more, or are you done?"

Robin reaches for her shopping bag. "I've got everything I came for. How about you? Do you need anything?"

I shake my head. "I just want to get out of here. I need to have a conversation with Chad, as uncomfortable as that's going to be."

"Do you want me to come over? Just in case it doesn't go as planned." She peers at me with a concerned look.

"No. I'll let him know I showed you the letter. That way, if anything happens to me, the cops will know exactly who to come after."

Robin gives a nervous chuckle. We walk in relative silence out to the parking lot where she hugs me tightly in parting. "Call me as soon as you've had that conversation with Chad. I want to know how it goes."

"I will, and don't worry about me. If I seriously thought my husband had anything to do with Shana's death, or Laura's disappearance, I wouldn't go home right now. Even the police didn't believe Laura's theory about Chad killing Shana, so what does that tell you?"

On the drive home, I go over in my mind how best to broach the subject with Chad. Robin said to test him, and that's not a bad idea to give me some peace of mind.

Chad's still out golfing when I arrive home, so I kick off my shoes and curl up on the couch to watch a little television.

I tense and mute the volume when I hear the sound of the garage door opening.

"Hey, how was the shopping trip?" Chad asks, strolling into the kitchen a few minutes later.

"Uneventful. How was golf?"

He flaps a hand at me. "Not my best day. I need to run upstairs and grab my phone. I forgot to take it with me."

Seconds later, he comes thundering back down the stairs.

My heart leaps up my throat when I see the strangled look on his face. "What's wrong?"

"Mom messaged me."

32

I stare at Chad, my chest tightening as I wait for him to read the text from his mother. So much for her being dead.

"She's going to be traveling in her camper for the next two months," he says, looking up from his phone. "She won't be in touch, but she's willing to reconcile when she gets back, if you feel ready to apologize by then."

I toss the remote aside and spring to my feet. "Are you kidding me? She made us cut our honeymoon short by threatening to commit suicide, and now she's taking off for two months instead of meeting with us."

Chad shakes his head. "I don't know what to tell you. It's unacceptable. I'll text her back right now."

"Wait! Before you do that, I need to show you something."

He hesitates, his finger hovering over his phone screen as I fish Laura's letter out of my purse. It's time Chad knew the full extent of the insanity we're dealing with.

"This was delivered to my office by courier," I say, handing him the letter. "I don't know what frame of mind your mother is in, but she appears to be living in alternate realities. You might want to read this before you respond to her text."

Chad takes the letter from me, a puzzled expression on his face. He sinks down on the couch and begins to read.

I pace back-and-forth across the room impatiently waiting for him to get to the end. I need to know what he makes of her latest claim to be dead. I can't even imagine what he must be feeling reading his mother's accusations about him. Surely this will be enough to induce him to break off his relationship with her entirely. Or maybe he'll just feel sorry for her in her delusional state.

After a minute or two, he lets out a weighty sigh and tosses the letter aside. He rubs a hand over his jaw. "It's all nonsense, you do realize that, don't you?"

"Yes," I say, somewhat unconvincingly.

Chad blinks at me, an injured expression on his face. "Do you actually think I'm capable of murdering someone, let alone my own mother?"

"No, of course not. But she has my mind in knots. When she mentioned the life insurance, it made me think of our conversation in Maui. I just need some reassurance from you that this letter is a bunch of baloney."

Chad walks over to me and places his hands on my shoulders. He looks me intently in the eye. "The only reason Shana and I took out life insurance policies was because we loved each other so much we didn't want to leave the other one in the lurch if anything were to happen—which, tragically, it did. I only suggested we do the same because you were so nervous about that helicopter ride—it reminded me how fickle life is. I don't want you to be stressed out if anything were to happen to me. I couldn't care less about the money. We can forget the whole idea of life insurance if that makes you feel better. Or we can just take out a policy on me. I want to do whatever eases your mind."

He presses me to his chest and caresses the back of my head. My stress begins to melt away and I relax a little. After a few minutes, he releases me. "I'm sorry about that obnoxious letter. I don't know if she's having some kind of psychotic episode, or what's going on, but this isn't the mother I know. She hasn't been the same since Shana died."

I pick the letter up and peruse it once more. "What happened to Shana's jewelry?"

Chad rubs the back of his neck. "She was wearing it when she was found. The police returned it to me. A few weeks after the funeral, her mother and sister came to the house to help me go through her things. I told them they were welcome to take her jewelry. It was too painful for me to keep it, but I wanted to give it to someone who would treasure it."

I nod, unsure what to say. It's not a story I can verify, but it sounds plausible. Personally, I wouldn't have parted with my husband's wedding ring, but everyone feels differently about these things.

"I'll get rid of this letter. No need for anyone else to know about it," I say. I'm not going to mention that I already showed it to Robin. It will only upset him.

"So, where do we go from here?" I ask.

Chad sets his lips in a stiff grimace. "We carry on with our lives. Without her. There will be no reconciliation when she returns from her travels."

33

Seven weeks later

I stare at the pregnancy test in disbelief. Chad and I wanted to start trying for a baby right away, but, at thirty-six, I never imagined I would become pregnant so quickly. A range of emotions surge through me. I'm more than ready for this new chapter of life, but it also complicates things. The truth is, I'm afraid of the grandmother of my unborn child, and dreading her return. If she hates me, will she hate my baby also? Or will she see it as Chad's child and demand to play a role in its life? No doubt, she'll view me as an obstacle to whatever it is she wants. If I was in danger before, I'm in twice as much danger now.

I can't help daydreaming at work about what the future holds with a child in it. I know Chad will be a wonderful dad, but he comes with strings attached. The wicked witch is still not out of the picture—either that, or she's haunting me from beyond the grave. With the threat of her return imminent, I need to make sure Chad and I are still on the same page about cutting off all contact.

"What are you mindlessly grinning about?" Rose asks, stopping by my desk with a stack of files in her arms. "Did you get a promotion or something I have yet to hear about?"

I force a laugh. I'm not ready to tell her about my pregnancy yet. It will be megaphoned all over the office in half a heartbeat. "I'm just thinking about how happy I've been for the past few weeks with Chad's mother out of the picture. I'm not looking forward to her return next week."

"Do you have any idea where she went?" Rose asks.

"No. And neither do her kids. She refuses to tell them anything. I think she enjoys keeping everyone in the dark." I give a ghost of a smile. "She's going to have a shock when she returns. Chad has agreed to sever all ties with her. And I didn't have to strong arm him into it. There's no coming back from what she's done this time."

Rose raises her eyebrows. "Oh? Did I miss something?"

"She wrote a nasty letter accusing Chad of all sorts of things he didn't do. I burned it in the fireplace. I'm sick of her malicious lies. He's had enough of her now, too."

"I don't blame him," Rose says. "Although, if you ask me, he should have kicked her to the curb a long time ago. The way she treated you from the get-go was appalling."

"At least she didn't succeed in her bid to drive us apart. Chad and I are stronger now than ever."

WHEN I CLOCK out of work later that afternoon, I text Brandy and Robin to see if they're available for a drink—Chad's working the late shift tonight so he won't be home until midnight. I'll only be able to have a mocktail, but I want to share my good news and brainstorm some ideas for a unique way to let Chad know we're expecting. I did a little browsing on the internet and almost ordered him a *best dad ever* mug, but it's kind of lame. I want to come up with something more fun.

Thirty minutes later, I'm sitting in our favorite bar with an umbrella in my drink, waiting on Brandy and Robin to arrive. I know they'll be thrilled for me and Chad—I only hope they don't read it on my face right away. I want to be able to surprise them. They arrive within minutes of each other and join me at the table.

"I'm glad you texted," Brandy says, shrugging off her coat. "I had plans with friends, but they fell through at the last minute."

"What are you drinking?" Robin asks me.

"Peach Margarita. It's delicious." I'm keeping the fact that it's alcohol free to myself for now.

The girls head off to order their drinks and come back a couple of minutes later with strawberry daiquiris in hand.

"I thought about trying your peach concoction," Robin says, "but I've never been a big fan of peaches."

"I talked her into the daiquiri," Brandy says, letting out a satisfied sigh. "Yum! Just what the doctor ordered."

"How was work?" Robin asks, reaching for her glass.

"The usual. Frantic lawyers running around the office barking out requests for case files and evidence—scrambling to get everything ready for court."

Brandy shakes her head. "I don't know how you do it. It sounds so stressful. I'll take my job in the library any day—bookworms are a pretty placid bunch for the most part."

I laugh. "You get used to the hectic pace. But I didn't want to get together with you guys to gripe about work. I have something to tell you."

Both heads snap toward me as they clutch their drinks in anticipation.

"I'm pregnant," I say, unable to stop the dam of happiness from breaking over my face.

Robin shrieks and wraps me up in a hug. "Yay! I'm going to be an aunt!"

It's only when she releases me that I realize Brandy is crying.

34

"Brandy! What's wrong?" I ask, reaching out a hand and resting it on her shoulder.

She shakes her head, dabbing at her eyes. "I'm sorry. Don't mind me. These are tears of joy, really."

I shoot Robin a questioning look. Her expression matches my gut feeling. There's more to this than meets the eye.

"Brandy, you can speak freely with us," I say. "I know something's bothering you. I didn't mean to upset you by—"

"It's not your fault," she interrupts, attempting to smile at me through her tears. "I'm genuinely delighted for you. It was just a shock, that's all." She drops her gaze and picks at her sleeve. "The thing is, I can't have kids of my own."

I suck in my breath and wait for her to elaborate, but she doesn't say anything more. I can't help wondering if this is why she never dates. I've offered to set her up with someone from work on multiple occasions, but she always says she isn't interested.

"I'm so sorry, Brandy," I offer. "I had no idea. Chad never said anything."

"Guys don't like to talk about these kinds of things," she says. She reaches for her cocktail with trembling fingers and takes a small sip. "It makes Chad uncomfortable."

"They're coming up with new infertility breakthroughs all the time, "Robin chimes in. "Maybe there's still a possibility."

Brandy pulls out another tissue and blows her nose. " Sadly, not for me. She flaps a dismissive hand. "Anyway, enough about me. I didn't mean to ruin the moment for you. I'm as bad as my mother." She brushes away her tears and smiles at me. "I can't wait to be an aunt, although I should probably warn you, Robin and I are going to spoil this little bean rotten."

Robin laughs. "You'd better believe it. You know how much I love to shop."

I take a sip of my mocktail, grinning over the rim of my glass at the two of them. "You're the first people I've told. I haven't mentioned it to anyone at work. Rose's lips flap faster than a hummingbird's wings, and I don't want the whole office knowing. And I haven't told Chad yet, either."

Robin's eyes widen. "How long are you going to keep him in the dark?"

"Not long. I'm too excited to keep it to myself, but I wanted to get your input on how I should tell him. I want to do something unique and original. Any ideas?"

"How about writing a message on your belly—like, *hi daddy,* or something to that effect?" Robin suggests.

"Or you could put a newborn onesie in his underwear drawer and tell him there's a surprise in it for him," Brandy says, tracing a finger around the rim of her glass.

"Cute! I like both those suggestions," I say. "Keep them coming."

We continue throwing around ideas for the next half

hour or so, laughing hysterically at some of the far-fetched schemes we come up with. I'm relieved to see that Brandy seems to have recovered from her emotional meltdown earlier. I can't imagine how difficult it must be knowing she'll never have kids of her own. My heart goes out to her, but I'm more worried now than ever about Laura's return next week. If her daughter can't have children, then I'm her only hope for a grandchild.

There's no telling how she'll respond to the news of my pregnancy.

35

The following day after work I swing by our local bakery to pick up a chocolate fudge cake—Chad's favorite. Thankfully, I'm not feeling nauseous so far in this pregnancy, so I intend to indulge as well. After going back-and-forth on a couple of suggestions from Robin and Brandy, I settled on the idea of hiding a pacifier in Chad's slice of cake. I can't wait to see his face when he discovers it. I wonder if he'll realize the significance of it or if I'll have to spell it out for him.

When I arrive home, I hide the cake in the pantry and set about making dinner—shrimp pasta in a cream sauce. Excitement ripples over my shoulders when I hear the sound of the front door opening.

"Hey honey," Chad calls to me, as he strides into the kitchen. He walks over to the stove where I'm stirring the sauce, and slips his arms around my waist. I tense, wondering if it's possible my belly could give me away, but I quickly dismiss the ridiculous notion. The baby's not even the size of a jellybean yet.

"How was work?" I ask, trying to nail a casual tone as I add more cream to the sauce.

"Stressful. I had one guy who coded this afternoon."

"Ugh, did he make it?"

"No. We couldn't save him, unfortunately. He wasn't that old either."

"I'm so sorry, honey," I say, turning to hug him.

"Me too," Chad says. "It's always worse when they're young."

I start dishing up the pasta and spoon the sauce over it. I'm glad I have some good news to share to lighten the mood.

Chad carries the plates into the dining room.

"Candles?" He raises his brows. "Please don't tell me it's our anniversary and I forgot all about it."

I laugh. "You know it's not our anniversary. I just thought it would be nice to have a romantic evening."

He eyes me with an air of apprehension. "Are you nervous about my mother returning next week?"

I shrug. "Not much I can do about it, so I'm not going to worry about it."

"She can't get into the house now that we've changed the locks," Chad says, reaching for his fork. "And I'm not going to resume a relationship with her. Not after that letter full of disgusting lies."

'I take it she hasn't contacted you since," I say.

"No. She won't respond to Brandy's messages anymore either. Brandy's pretty hurt about it."

"Your mother's sick and twisted." I say.

Chad chews on a shrimp, looking uncomfortable at the sentiment.

"Why don't we change the subject?" I suggest. "Let's talk about where we want to go on vacation this year."

We fall into a comfortable back-and-forth chat, and the rest of the dinner goes off without a hitch. After clearing away the dishes, I tell Chad to sit back down at the table. "I picked up a fudge cake for dessert. Would you like a coffee with yours?"

"Sure, that sounds great," he replies.

I brew some coffee, then cut two generous slices of cake and stuff the pacifier underneath one of them. It looks a little misshapen but not too noticeable. I load everything onto a tray and carry it into the dining room.

"Thanks, honey," Chad says, as I hand him a plate. "This looks delicious."

I chew on a mouthful of cake, my eyes never leaving Chad. He eats a couple of bites, then stabs his fork into the middle of his cake. "What on earth is that?"

He frowns and holds his plate up to inspect the cake more closely. "There's something in my piece. Where did you get this cake from?"

"Our local bakery," I say with an innocent shrug. "What is it?"

Chad pokes his fork in the cake again and begins scraping the pacifier free. "I don't believe this. It's a child's pacifier. That's so gross. How on earth did they drop something like that into the batter. You need to get a refund. I mean—"

He breaks off mid-sentence when he catches me grinning.

"The bakery didn't put the pacifier in there, Chad—I did."

He blinks at me, flummoxed at first, then realization dawns in his eyes. "You're ... you're pregnant?"

I nod, smiling so hard my cheeks ache. "I wanted to tell you last night, but you were working late."

"Eva!" Chad jumps to his feet and squeezes me tightly. "I can't believe it happened so quickly. I'm over the moon. We're going to find out what we're having, aren't we? Please don't keep me in suspense for nine months. I don't think I could stand it."

"I'd just as soon have a surprise," I say, "but we can find out if you want to. It will make shopping for the munchkin easier."

Chad straightens up and rubs his chin, frowning. "We'll need to revisit that life insurance policy now that we have a child on the way. It's not an option anymore."

His eyes lock like a laser with mine, and a cold shiver fingers its way down my spine.

36

C had picks up the pacifier and licks the frosting off it. "We're keeping this treasure. One day we'll present it to the kiddo and tell him or her the story of how you broke the news of your pregnancy to me."

I give him an unsettled smile. Was I overreacting to the intensity I saw in his eyes a moment ago when he brought up the life insurance policies again? *It's not an option anymore.* Maybe it was just the realization that he's going to become a father that made him so impassioned. I try to shake my misgivings, but it's hard not to wonder again if there's any truth to Laura's letter. It could have been just the protector in Chad talking, or he could have been seizing on this opportunity to insist on what he wanted all along. I'm not sure all the secrets in the Turner family have surfaced yet. I need to proceed with caution.

"Why didn't you tell me that Brandy couldn't have kids?" I ask, thinking back to my conversation in the pub with her and Robin.

Chad raises a sharp eyebrow. "Who told you that?"

"Brandy did. When I broke the news to her and Robin

last night that I was pregnant, she started crying. When I asked her what was wrong, she told us she was infertile."

A sheen of sweat appears on Chad's forehead. "Did she ... say anything else?"

"What do you mean?"

He shrugs. "I don't know. I guess I'm just worried that your pregnancy is going to hit her hard."

I nod. "It won't be easy for her. How about we ask her to be our baby's godmother? I know she'll be a wonderful aunt, and we'll make sure to involve her as much as we can in our kiddo's life."

"What about Robin?" Chad asks.

"She won't mind in the least. She'll support our decision —she saw how broken Brandy was when she told us she couldn't have kids."

Chad reaches for my hand and squeezes it. "Thanks Eva. I know Brandy will appreciate that."

I twist my lips. "Your mother, on the other hand, is not allowed anywhere near our baby."

"Agreed. We won't even tell her about the pregnancy, or she'll keep texting me the entire time begging to see the baby when it's born."

I wrinkle my forehead in thought. "That's the part I'm most worried about. I can protect our baby for now, but your mother is deranged. What if she tries to snatch it after it's born?"

A look of horror crosses Chad's face. "We'll have to make sure she never gets near enough to do that. She can't get into our house anymore, and Brandy changed the code on her house too. She doesn't want Mom in there without her knowledge anymore either."

"I've been thinking a lot about that letter she sent through her lawyer," I say. "I've been wondering how she came up with the idea that Shana was pushed—what if she killed her?"

Chad throws me an alarmed look. "Why would she do that? She loved Shana."

"That was the impression she gave everybody. But five million dollars is a lot of money. And, to be fair, you paid off Laura's mortgage with some of it."

"She didn't ask me to do that."

I shrug. "She didn't have to. She knew you would offer."

Chad shakes his head slowly in a disbelieving fashion. " You're making a very serious accusation, Eva. That's a stretch—even after everything that's happened. I'd be the first to admit that my mother has become petty and spiteful since Shana's death, but she's not a murderer."

"You don't know that for sure. You said yourself she might be having some kind of psychotic episode." I take his hands in mine. "What if that bloody knife at my bridal shower was a cry for help. *Beware the killer among you.* What if she was talking about herself?"

37

I register the shock on Chad's face as my words sink in. Shana's autopsy didn't show any signs of foul play, but it's only to be expected if someone pushed her off the hiking trail. Suspicion would never fall on Laura—she went out of her way to foster a great relationship with her daughter-in-law.

"I just don't know what her motivation would have been," Chad says. "You brought up the life insurance, but it's not as if she inherited the policy."

I take a steadying breath before stating the obvious. "Not yet. But everything you have was left to her in your will, up until we got married."

"So what are you saying? That she was planning on killing me too?"

"Possibly. It would explain her hatred of me. I came on the scene and thwarted her plans. I'm standing between her and the money. She's not going to see a penny of it unless she gets rid of us both."

Chad shakes his head. "I don't buy it, Eva. It's too fantastical. This isn't some crime thriller made for TV. This is my mother you're talking about. How is she supposed to murder the two of us and get away with it?"

"I don't know. Maybe that's what this extended trip was all about," I say. "She could have been plotting something—trying to hire a hitman for all we know."

Chad rubs a hand uneasily across his jaw. "Eva, you're starting to sound unhinged."

"Am I? All I can tell you is that when she rolls into town next week, she'd better not show her face anywhere near me, or she'll regret it."

THE FOLLOWING week goes by with no sign of Laura returning, and no further communication with her, despite repeated attempts by Brandy to message and call.

"I reported her missing again," Brandy announces, when she comes over to the house one evening to discuss the situation with Chad and me.

I hand her a mug of coffee. "Do you think the police will take it seriously this time?"

"I hope so. No one has heard from her in weeks. The police should at least check if her credit cards have been used, or if she's withdrawn money from her bank accounts."

"Do you really think something might have happened to her?" I ask.

Brandy twirls a strand of hair around her finger. "We have to consider the possibility that she might have harmed herself. She's been behaving erratically."

"What did you make of that bloody knife at the bridal shower?" Chad asks.

Brandy looks perturbed. "I don't know. I wanted Eva to report it to the police at the time."

"She thinks Mom was behind it," Chad says.

"I just wondered if it might have been a cry for help," I explain. "That 'beware the killer among you' message might have been a reference to herself."

Brandy eyes us dubiously. "So, Mom was trying to tell us she was afraid she might kill you? That sounds psycho to me."

Chad sighs. "Eva thinks she might have killed before."

"What?" Brandy's eyes swivel in my direction.

"It's just a theory," I say. "Before she left on her trip, she sent me a letter accusing Chad of pushing Shana into the ravine. I know it was just another attempt to drive us apart, but where did she even come up with the idea?"

Brandy's eyes grow wide as saucers. "Why would she want to do away with Shana?"

Chad's shoulders sag. "Maybe for the life insurance money. I paid off her mortgage, and I've been helping her out with other miscellaneous things since. Whatever the reason, she's clearly unstable. She changed after Shana's death. What I'm trying to figure out is if she's more of a danger to us or to herself."

Brandy winces. "Do you really think she would hurt her own children?"

"In a heartbeat," I say. "I think her plan was to get rid of Chad before I came on the scene. She stands to inherit his estate. But I complicated things. It's a lot harder to kill two people and make it look like an accident."

The color drains from Brandy's face. "But ... she adores Chad. He's her biological child."

I frown, not understanding the point she's trying to make. I throw a questioning look in Chad's direction. A hint of irritation crosses his face.

"Mom and Dad tried for almost a decade to have kids,

before they adopted Brandy," he explains. "A couple of months after that, Mom got pregnant with me."

"You never told me that," I say in an accusing tone. I'm frustrated to be constantly finding out, purely by accident, things I should know about the Turners. I'm surprised Brandy didn't tell me either, but maybe it's another sensitive topic for her.

Chad shrugs. "It was never important to us. Brandy and I were always brother and sister, and that's all that matters."

I want to tell him that it matters to me that he kept the information from me. We're married now and we shouldn't have secrets.

It makes me feel like there could be other things he's keeping from me.

38

The thought hangs with me like a throbbing hangnail. Do I know the man I married—the father of my child? I thought we had shared everything with each other, but things are beginning to trickle out I knew nothing about. Granted, nothing that would have stopped me from marrying him. But that's not the point. There are still things he should have shared with me.

I spend a restless night tossing and turning as I mull over how much my pregnancy has changed my outlook on all of this. My chief goal now is to protect my child from danger no matter where it lurks—especially if that danger lurks within the Turner family. Do I trust my husband? Yes, but not wholeheartedly. I still feel the need to verify some things. We haven't merged our bank accounts, so I have no idea about his current financial state of affairs. I know how much he got in the life insurance payout, but I don't know what he did with it—other than paying off the mortgages. I don't know where the rental properties are that he bought. Supposedly, he has a property manager who looks after them. And I'm curious about his will. He told me he altered it to make me the sole beneficiary, but what if that was a lie? He's never actually shown me the paperwork, and I never felt the need to ask for proof.

I hate the idea of snooping on my husband, but if that's what it's going to take to give me some peace of mind, then that's what I'll do. He's working the late shift at the hospital again this evening, so I'll have plenty of time after work to investigate—starting with his laptop. The problem will be cracking his password.

I spend every spare minute I have at work that day googling how to decipher someone's computer password. Turns out there are open source offline password-cracking tools available but, after reading up on the topic, I realize I'm not tech savvy enough to figure it out. My best bet is to try several combinations of dates that he might have used.

"Chad's working late tonight, isn't he?" Rose says, leaning on my desk. "Want to grab some tacos?"

"I, um ... can't. I have chores waiting for me at home."

Rose rolls her eyes. "So what? Guaranteed, they're not going anywhere."

"Rain check," I say, winking at her as I slip the strap of my purse over my shoulder. I hurry out of the office before she can try another tack to persuade me to join her.

Chad calls me on the way home, and I almost don't pick up. I'm afraid he might hear something in my voice that will alert him to the fact that something's wrong. But if I don't answer, it will make him more concerned—especially now that I'm pregnant.

"Hey honey," I say.

"How are you feeling?"

"Fine." I chuckle. "Like I told you, no nausea. I'm one of the lucky ones."

"That's great," he says. "I don't want to put a damper on

your evening, but Brandy just called me. Mom finally messaged her."

My heart sinks. I'm tired of this endless game of now you see me, now you don't. "What did she have to say this time?"

"She's coming back into town on Saturday. She wants us all to go over there on Sunday for lunch."

"Not going to happen. We agreed to cut her off, remember?"

"Right," Chad says. "That's what I told Brandy. She said she'll go over there by herself and try and reason with her. She'll bring me up to speed afterward."

I suddenly feel a little queasy in my stomach as an image of that bloody knife flashes to mind. I don't like the idea of Brandy going over to her mom's place alone. *Beware the killer among you.*

If Laura even suspects for one minute that Brandy's taking Chad's side of things, she might take a knife to her instead.

39

The minute I get home, I call Brandy. "I'm not comfortable with you going over to your mom's alone," I say. "But I don't want Chad going there either. How about you meet her someplace where there are other people around to defuse the situation, if need be?"

Brandy gives a nervous chuckle. "Why? You don't really think she would hurt me, do you? She's my mom."

"Is she any more? Chad doesn't recognize the person she's become."

"I really think she's tired of her huff-fest shenanigans. She wants to come back into our lives."

"I'll bet she does—on her terms," I add, with a hard edge in my tone. "It doesn't work that way."

"I'm not going to let her steamroll me, if that's what you're worried about, and I'm not going to give her a pass on her behavior either," Brandy says. "I'll let you know where she stands on the whole apology thing, but I'll make it clear to her that she's the one who needs to be apologizing."

"I think you're wasting your time, but I get it—she's still your mother at the end of the day."

Brandy lets out a long sigh. "Let's see where her mind's at after some time away to think about all the trouble she's caused. But enough about her. What's on your agenda this evening?"

I gulp back a startled breath, almost as though she's caught me in the act of trying to break into her brother's computer. It doesn't feel right to tell her what I'm up to. "Uh, nothing much. Just chilling."

"Are you feeling more tired than usual with the pregnancy?" she asks.

I hesitate for a minute, not wanting to say the wrong thing and trigger her pain. But I also want to be open to sharing the experience with her to whatever extent I can. "A little. I'm doing pretty well on the whole. No nausea, at least."

"Are you going to find out what you're having?"

I let out a bark of laughter. "Chad's like a little kid waiting on Christmas, so yes."

"I don't blame him," Brandy says. "The suspense would kill me. Have you talked about names yet?"

"No, we haven't had time with his crazy shifts. Maybe this weekend. Why don't you come over after you visit your mom and you can help us narrow down some names?"

"Really?" Brandy says, her voice barely more than a tremulous whisper.

"Yes, really!" I assure her. "We want you to be our child's godmother so you should be part of the naming process."

"I can't tell you how much that means to me," Brandy says, sounding as though she's struggling to hold back tears. "I'm going to get together with Robin and throw you the best baby shower ever. And this time my mother won't be invited."

"Please don't tell her I'm pregnant," I say, panic fluttering in my stomach.

"Definitely not!" Brandy assures me.

I hang up and wander into the kitchen to find something in the refrigerator to eat. I rarely cook on the nights Chad works late. I make myself a grilled cheese and heat up some leftover vegetable soup, then sit down at the table and open up Chad's laptop.

As I spoon the soup mindlessly into my mouth, I mull over the most likely password he would use. Robin uses her dog's name, but Chad and I don't have a pet so that rules that out. I'm guessing he would be more likely to use numbers—a date of some kind. I can't mess up too many times or I'll be locked out. I take a bite of my grilled cheese, then punch in my birthday, followed by Chad's birthday, followed by our wedding date. No joy. Surely he wouldn't use his mother's birthday—I shiver, repulsed at the thought. I don't want her in our lives in any shape or form anymore— not even in a password. Somewhere at the back of my mind I recall Chad mentioning that his mother used Brandy's birthdate for everything. Is it possible he's using the same password?

I fish my phone from my purse and double check Brandy's birthday—April 25. It's worth a try. I don't have any better ideas. I take another bite of my sandwich, then type it in, almost choking when the screen flashes to life. Instinctively, I throw a glance over my shoulder as though someone might be watching. But there's no one there, of course. I push my plate aside, and pull the laptop toward me, trying to decide where to look first. I'm uncomfortable at the thought of going through Chad's emails, but it seems the logical next step. I need to know if there has been any communication between him and his mother.

My soup turns cold as I weed through Chad's inbox and deleted emails folder. I can't find any recent correspondence from Laura. I do a cursory search of his files, but I don't see anything incriminating there either. Frustrated, I pull up his search history and start browsing the tabs, stopping in my tracks a moment later. *Ethylene glycol.* Why on earth was Chad searching for ethylene glycol? Does it have something to do with his job? My chest tightens as I begin to read.

Ethylene glycol breaks down into toxic compounds in the body affecting the central nervous system, heart, and kidneys.

Ingesting enough can cause death.

The room seems to be tilting around me as I try to rationalize what I'm seeing on the page. I can't let my mind take a deep dive into the chasm of the unthinkable. Chad might have been researching something for a case he had at the hospital. I go back to his search history and scan through some of the other links he was browsing: *carbon monoxide, plant poisons, botulinum toxins, arsenic.* He was definitely researching poisons, for some reason or another.

My heart is racing so fast I'm afraid I'm going to pass out. Was Laura telling the truth in her letter after all? Was my husband planning on poisoning me before he found out about the baby? Surely he wouldn't kill his own child. I squeeze my head between my hands, forcing myself to think rationally. Chad loves me. There's no way he would hurt me. But that leaves just one conclusion.

He must have killed his mother.

40

I get up from the table and attempt to carry my dishes over to the sink. My hands are trembling so violently the soup bowl almost slides off the plate. I don't know what to do about what I've discovered on Chad's computer. Should I call the police? They're hardly going to take me seriously if I tell them I think my husband killed his mother. They're tired of Laura and her disappearing acts. She's cried wolf one too many times. Besides, there's no evidence that she's dead—other than my hormonal imagination. As a nurse, Chad's search history could be legitimate. There might be any number of reasons why he was researching poisons. If I'm way off base, I could jeopardize his job with false allegations.

I clutch my phone tightly in the palm of my hand, fearful I'll drop it before I manage to hit the speed dial for Robin's number. It rings and rings and goes to voicemail. She must be at work. As a manager of a busy restaurant, she can't take my call during her shift. I could text her, but I don't want to worry her. I rub a hand over my sweating brow.

I don't need this kind of stress right now. It can't be good for the baby.

I chew on my thumbnail, wondering what to do. Martina's on a cruise in the Caribbean somewhere. I could call Cindi, but she's so far away there's not much she can do to help me. Besides, we're not really in each other's lives anymore, and she doesn't understand the situation. That leaves Brandy as my only feasible option. But how on earth can I tell her that I think her brother might have killed their mother? It was crazy enough to suggest that Laura was a killer.

I sink back down at the table, my legs wobbling beneath me. What if Chad was the one who hid the bloody knife among my shower gifts? Maybe it had nothing to do with me—what if he was trying to send a message to his mother? She might have confronted him about her suspicions, and the knife was a warning to her to back off. My mind is going in circles, my thoughts spinning helplessly in a vortex of confusion. None of it makes much sense. I need to talk this over with someone—anyone.

My finger hovers over Rose's number. I'm tempted to dial it. I know she'd come over here in a heartbeat. But the story would be in the local news by the morning. She's the last person I should be bouncing my crazy conspiracy theories off. I'm out of options. Either I figure this out on my own—at least until I can get a hold of Robin—or I call Brandy and tell her what I found. I don't have to draw any conclusions over the phone. I just need to know what she makes of it.

I pull Chad's laptop toward me once again. I should take some pictures of the search results in case Chad clears them. My hand is shaking so badly it takes me several attempts and, even then, the shots are blurred when I scroll through them.

There are more searches on ethylene glycol than any of the other poisons, which leads me to conclude that Chad has settled on a method of choice, if murder is indeed what he has in mind. *A clear, odorless, sweet tasting liquid.* In other words, undetectable—which makes for the perfect crime.

The question is, how many perfect crimes has my husband committed?

41

I'm about to dial Brandy's number when I change my mind and decide to drive over to her house instead. I need to be able to look her in the face when I tell her what I've discovered. I want to know if she suspected anything—if she had a hunch all along that it was Chad who left the bloody knife at my shower, knowing I would blame their mother.

I shoot Brandy a quick text to make sure she's home, and ask if I can stop by.

Her reply comes through a moment later.

Sure. I picked up food if you're hungry.

I tap out a quick response. *Already ate, thanks. See you in a few.*

After closing up Chad's laptop, I position it exactly as he left it.

Despite my muddled thoughts, I do my best to remain calm on the drive to Brandy's. The last thing I need is to slam into the back of the vehicle in front of me at a stoplight because I'm trying to work out if my mother-in-law's a killer, or if she's been killed by my husband, or if Chad's planning to kill me.

Twenty minutes later, I pull up outside Brandy's house. I suck in an icy breath, hoping I'm doing the right thing. I might be completely off base. Brandy might hate me for even thinking such a thing about her brother, but how can she possibly explain the searches on his computer? It's not as if Laura could have snuck in there and set him up. Chad and I changed all the locks after she left.

Brandy greets me with a warm smile when she opens the door. I flash her a token smile in return, my stomach churning with apprehension. She has no idea what I'm about to hit her with. And I have no idea how she'll react.

"I'm glad you stopped by," Brandy says, curling up on the couch with a mug of hot tea in her hand. "I was just channel surfing looking for a new show to watch. Seen anything good lately?"

I frown, caught off guard by the banality of the question when I've been wading through landmines in my head for the past few hours. "Not really. I fall asleep every time I sit down in front of the television, and it has nothing to do with being pregnant."

Brandy laughs. "I know the feeling. We must be getting old."

I shift uncomfortably in my chair. I'm not sure how to broach the subject. I didn't have a legitimate reason to spy on Chad to begin with, other than a gut feeling.

"Eva, are you okay?" Brandy asks, raising her brows in concern. "Do you want another cushion or something?"

I shake my head. "No. I'm fine, thanks. Actually, I wanted to run something by you."

She rubs her hands together gleefully. "Let me guess, you have a name in mind."

"No. Nothing like that." I give a strained laugh. "I just need your opinion on something. I've been going around in circles in my mind, and I just want someone to tell me I'm overreacting."

Brandy cocks her head to one side. "I'm intrigued."

I take a deep breath, still unsure if I'm doing the right thing. "The battery went dead on my computer earlier," I begin. "I couldn't find my charging cord so I grabbed Chad's laptop. After an hour or so, I went into the history to find a tab I'd closed, only to discover a bunch of concerning searches." I take another steadying breath before continuing. "They were searches for undetectable poisons."

The crease between Brandy's brows deepens, but she says nothing, presumably waiting on me to continue.

"I guess I just wanted to know what you thought of that. I suppose it could have had something to do with his job, but it weirded me out. Most of the searches were for ethylene glycol. Apparently, it's a colorless, odorless liquid that tastes sweet so you wouldn't know if you were being poisoned with it."

Brandy's mouth drops open.

"I'm not suggesting Chad's trying to poison me," I hasten to add. "I just wondered about your mom—" I break off, unable to be honest about what I fear most—that the father of my child is a killer.

Brandy sets her mug aside, her face screwed up in concentration. "What date are these searches from?"

I pull up my phone and check the pictures I took of the websites. I was so freaked out when I found the searches that I didn't think to check the date. "It looks like they're all from a couple of months back."

Brandy sinks back on the couch. "Mom was still in town then. She had a key to your house."

"What are you saying?"

"I think she set Chad up. She wants you to think he's going to kill you so you'll leave him."

42

"My mother was the one who pushed Chad and Shana to take out the life insurance policies," Brandy says. "As the sole beneficiary, she stands to inherit everything."

I stare across at her, considering what she's saying. As shocking as it is, it makes perfect sense. Of course my husband isn't trying to kill me. His twisted mother has been trying to drive a wedge between us from the very beginning. She's like an invasive species infiltrating everything—impossible to eradicate, laying her trail of poison like a venomous ant for us to follow. She sent that letter knowing it would cause me to have doubts about Chad, hoping I would start snooping, like she suggested. Maybe she even thought I would divorce him and disappear from their lives, eradicating the need for her to get rid of me. But she doesn't know about the baby. And she doesn't know me very well. If she did, she would know I would fight to the bitter end for my family.

"You seem very sure that your mother's behind this," I say.

Brandy gives a hollow laugh, her face crumpling. "Sadly, yes. Chad's a prankster, but he's not a psycho."

I nod in agreement. "I know that. I guess I just needed to hear you say it too."

Brandy reaches for her tea. "I feel like I've reached the end of the line with Mom. Unless she has a dramatic change of heart on Sunday, I'm going to cut her off. I can't be in her life and in my niece or nephew's life at the same time. It's too dangerous. She's unstable."

I wet my lips, unsure if I should voice my agreement, even though I heartily second Brandy's decision. I won't allow my child to be anywhere in the vicinity of her crazy mother.

"Should I tell Chad about the search results I found on his laptop?" I ask.

Brandy shrugs. "If you want, but it will only reiterate how twisted our mother is, and bring him more pain."

"It might be enough to convince him that Laura killed Shana."

A pained expression crosses Brandy's face. "I guess we'll never know now, not unless she confesses."

I let out a scoffing laugh. "If she can't even apologize to me, she'll never confess to killing Shana."

Brandy blinks at me. I can almost see the gears clicking into motion in her head. "Maybe that's what we need to do," she says. "Get her to confess to Shana's murder."

I wrinkle my forehead. "How? That seems like an impossible task."

"She trusts me. What if I pretend to have fallen out with you and Chad? I could tell her I found the search history on Chad's computer and that I know she set him up, and I want to help. I'll record our conversation."

I pick at my sleeve, considering the idea. "You're

assuming she'll come clean with you. What if she denies everything?"

"Then we'll figure out something else. But knowing her, she's proud of what she's done—the bloody knife, the note, even Shana's death. She might admit to it all if she thinks I'm on her side."

"We'd still have to prove it," I point out.

"That's up to the police. But if I have a recorded confession, they'll be obligated to open up an investigation into Shana's death."

"Do you think she was planning on murdering Chad with the ethylene glycol?" I ask.

Brandy throws me a dark look. "I think she's going to try and get rid of us all."

43

Fear blisters over my skin at Brandy's words. If she's right, it's incredibly risky to pretend to align herself with her mother. Laura may be unhinged, but she's not stupid. If she smells a rat, Brandy could very well find herself drinking poison.

"I don't like this plan," I say. "You're putting yourself in danger."

"I'll take precautions," Brandy assures me. "I'm not going to risk eating or drinking anything while I'm at her house—not after the search history you showed me."

"How are you going to convince her that you had a falling out with Chad?" I ask. "She knows you two are close."

Her expression morphs into a stiff grimace. "I'll think of something. I could offer to help her get rid of him if she agrees to split the inheritance with me."

"I doubt that will convince her. We need to come up with a better reason for your sudden change of heart when it comes to your only sibling."

Brandy chews on her lip for a moment. "There is something else we could try, but I'm not sure how you'd feel about it."

"What?" I ask, eying her curiously.

"I could tell her you're pregnant. If she thinks there's someone else in line to collect the inheritance she's angling for, it will make her doubly desperate."

I twist my hands in my lap, a sinking feeling in my gut. It will make her doubly desperate, but also twice as dangerous. I'm not sure I'm willing to take that risk. "I need to talk it over with Chad first," I say.

"He'll never agree to it," Brandy says. "We both know he's not going to do anything that puts you and the baby in danger."

"Okay, we'll leave Chad out of it. Let me talk it over with Robin. I trust her judgment."

Brandy drains the rest of her tea. "Don't leave it too long. I'm still planning on going to Mom's on Sunday."

"I'll text Robin right now and have her swing by my place on her way home from work," I say, getting to my feet. "Chad's working the late shift, so he won't be back until two in the morning."

IT's ALMOST 11:00 p.m. by the time Robin finally shows up. She kicks off her shoes and throws herself down on the couch. "Phew! We were packed tonight. And the head chef was out sick. It was one fiasco after another all night long."

Ordinarily, I relish listening to her entertaining tales of demanding patrons and mutinous staff, but tonight I have more important things on my mind.

Sensing my silence, she straightens up and frowns at me. "What was it you wanted to talk to me about? Is everything okay with the baby?"

"Yes. All's good on that front." I take a deep breath and fill her in on what I discovered on Chad's computer.

She listens intently, her hand moving to cover her mouth at times. When I'm done talking, she lets out a long, low whistle. "I don't like the sound of that at all. I think you should come home with me tonight."

"Not so fast," I say. "I talked it over with Brandy. She doesn't think Chad conducted those searches. She's convinced Laura set him up. It's certainly possible. The searches are from a couple of months back when she still had a key to our place."

"But why would she set her own son up?"

"For the life insurance money. She persuaded Chad to take out hefty policies on himself and Shana, and Laura was named as the beneficiary, if anything were to happen to them—that is, until I came along. She needs to get rid of me, one way or another. It's easier to scare me off than murder me."

Robin picks at her nails, deep in thought. "I'm still not entirely convinced. What if Brandy's wrong?"

"About what?"

Robin blinks solemnly at me. "What if it turns out that Chad conducted those searches?"

My eyes jerk toward my sister. "What are you saying? Do you think Chad and his mother are in on it together?"

She tilts her head, considering this for a moment. "That's a possibility. But what if there's some truth to Laura's letter?"

I gasp. "*Some* truth? What parts do you think might be true?"

A grim expression settles on her face. "What if Chad really did kill Shana?" Her voice quiets to a whisper. "And what if Laura's dead?"

44

My brain feels like it's turning to mush. I'm not sure if it's the late hour, or the pregnancy hormones, or some combination of both, but I'm not tracking with Robin. "How can Laura be dead?" I ask, wrinkling my brow in confusion. "She invited us over on Sunday."

Robin inches forward to the edge of her chair. "Did she though?"

"Yes!" I reply indignantly. "I saw the message she sent Brandy and Chad."

"But if Chad killed Laura, he could be sending those messages from her phone," Robin persists.

The weight in the pit of my stomach grows heavier. I fleetingly entertain the thought, before dismissing it outright. It's preposterous to think my husband could have perpetrated such an elaborate fraud.

"They could have schemed together to kill Shana, then had a falling out when he met you," Robin goes on. "Or maybe they argued over how to divvy up the money. No matter. The point is, I'm not convinced Laura is even alive anymore." She hesitates, lasering her gaze on me. "How much do you want to bet she won't come home on Sunday either?"

An icy thread of panic ripples through me.

"You need to think long and hard about what you're going to do," Robin says. "You have to protect yourself. If I'm right that Laura's dead, you're in more danger than ever now that you're pregnant. So far, Brandy is sticking by Chad, but she's going to start asking some hard questions too, if her mother's a no show."

A line of sweat prickles on my brow.

"Unless she's in on it," Robin goes on. "Maybe it's a family affair."

"I doubt it. She's a bit naïve when it comes to her mother, and she has her brother on a pedestal. She was ecstatic at the thought of becoming an aunt to his child."

"So what are you going to do?" Robin asks.

I plant my feet on the floor and drag myself upright. "I'm exhausted. I'm going to bed. I'll confront Chad about what I found in the morning."

Robin's eyes swerve to me. "That's a really bad idea, Sis."

"I trust Chad," I say. "If he was really trying to poison me, he would have deleted his search history. Whoever conducted those searches on his computer wanted them to be found."

45

"I'm going to crash here tonight," Robin says. "There's no way I'm letting you confront Chad on your own, not if there's even the minutest chance he's a killer."

"He's not," I say. "I'm certain of that. What I'm not so sure about is whether he ever had any suspicions about his mother. I want to know if he covered up anything about Shana's death."

"If he did, he's an accessory to murder in the eyes of the law, and you'll have to turn him in." Robin arches a reproving brow at me. "Which means you'll be out of a husband."

"Thanks for sending me to bed with that comforting thought."

Robin stifles a yawn as she reaches for her shoes. "Somebody needs to tell it like it is."

"The guest bed's made up," I say. "And there are travel toiletries under the sink."

Robin pulls me in for a quick hug. "Thanks, Sis. Make sure you wake me when you get up. I want to be there with you when you confront Chad."

Even though I'm exhausted, I can't fall asleep. Every time I start to drift off, I jolt awake, terrified that my husband is hovering over me with a knife, or flexing a rope, or opening a bottle of pills to force down my throat. It's nonsense to think he could have killed his first wife and be planning on killing me too. This is all part of Laura's plot to mess with my mind, and it's working. It doesn't prove anything if she doesn't show up on Sunday. She revels in stringing us along and wreaking havoc on our lives.

I tense when I hear Chad's car pulling into the garage. Minutes later, I hear his footfall on the stairs. I lie like a statue beneath the sheets, eyes scrunched shut, face turned into the pillow. I can't let him know I'm awake. I'm too fraught with emotion to have the conversation I need to have with him right now. And I'm certainly not going to wake Robin at this time of night.

Chad pads into the bathroom, discarding his clothes in a trail as he goes. He leaves the door open and I hear the sound of the shower running. When he crawls into bed next to me minutes later, I try not to recoil from his warm body. He falls asleep almost instantly and I feel an immediate sense of relief mixed with a twinge of resentment at his ability to sleep regardless of what's going on in our lives.

I stare up at the ceiling, going over in my mind what I need to say to him. He certainly has some explaining to do, but what if he denies knowing anything about the online searches for poisons? Will he subscribe to Brandy's theory that his mother set him up?

At some point, I must have dozed off because I wake the following morning with a start. Chad is snoring lightly in bed next to me. I roll over and gingerly maneuver my way to the edge of the mattress and slide my feet to the floor. I manage to make it out of the bedroom without waking him, and I pull the door quietly closed behind me.

After tightening the belt on my robe, I head downstairs to brew some coffee. There's no sign of Robin yet, and I have no intention of waking her until Chad gets up. In the meantime, I'll sit with my coffee and try to figure out how to handle this on my own.

It's almost an hour later before my bleary-eyed husband stumbles downstairs.

"Hey, honey," he mumbles, kissing me on the forehead before traipsing over to the coffee maker. "I saw Robin's car parked at the curb."

"Yeah, she stopped by after work and ended up spending the night." I can hardly tell Chad she slept over because she suspects him of murder. "I promised I'd wake her," I say, getting to my feet. "She has to go home before she heads into work this afternoon."

"She's already up," he says, sitting down next to me at the counter. "I heard the shower going in the guest bathroom."

I curl my fingers around my mug, trying to quell the feeling of dread in my stomach. "Chad, there's something I need to ask you."

He raises his brows as he runs a hand through his hair. "Sounds ominous. Am I going to have to repaint a bedroom for this baby? You know how I feel about painting."

I tweak a smile. "I had to use your computer yesterday when my battery died. I had an important case to upload. I couldn't help noticing some really concerning searches for undetectable poisons—ethylene glycol in particular."

Chad rumples his brow, looking flummoxed. "I don't know what you're talking about."

Our heads swivel in the direction of the door as Robin strides into the room. She folds her arms in front of her and narrows her eyes at Chad. "What Eva wants to know is if you killed your mother?"

46

C had looks from Robin to me in bewilderment. "What are you two talking about?"

"Don't play games," Robin says. "You've been researching undetectable poisons on your computer. Quite the coincidence that nobody has seen your mother for a couple of months, not to mention the fact that your first wife—"

"Robin! Please!" I cut in. "At least give him a chance to explain himself."

Chad rams his fingers into his hair and stares at Robin with a crazed expression on his face. "Are you out of your mind? Do you really think I'd kill my own mother?" He turns to me. "What are these searches you're talking about? Show me!"

I fetch his laptop from the counter where he left it and hand it to him. "Check your history. You'll see what I'm talking about."

He sits down at the table and opens up his laptop, an injured expression on his face. He taps on the keyboard for a couple of minutes, the crease between his brows deepening as he studies the screen. "What is this?" he asks, throwing up his hands. "I don't know anything about these searches. Someone's been on my computer."

Robin rolls her eyes. "And who would that have been? Are you suggesting my sister suddenly developed an interest in poisons?" She marches over to the table and rests her hands on the back of a chair, glaring at Chad. "Did you kill Shana for the life insurance?"

His jaw drops open. "How dare you! What happened to Shana was a tragic accident, and it broke my heart."

I tug on Robin's sleeve. "Calm down, Sis. This isn't getting us anywhere. It's obvious Chad doesn't know anything about the searches. Laura has to be behind this. She set him up."

"Why would she do that?" Chad asks.

I shrug. "To drive a wedge between us and make me think you killed your first wife. Maybe she wanted to scare me into thinking I was next. She told me to search your computer in that letter she sent. She wanted me to find those searches."

Chad runs a hand over his stubble. "I can't let Brandy go over to Mom's on Sunday alone. I won't let her be the sacrificial lamb."

"Then I guess you need to talk her out of it, because you're not, under any circumstances, going with her."

A haunted look crosses his face. "What if Mom did have something to do with Shana's death? I can't ignore the possibility after everything that's transpired."

"She'll never admit to it," Robin says. "And there's no way to prove it."

"Maybe not. But we can stop her from killing again," Chad says.

"How?" I ask. "The police aren't going to do anything based on a hunch we have."

"We're going to do their job for them," Chad replies, a gleam of satisfaction in his eyes. "We'll set a trap and watch her walk right into it."

47

"What kind of a trap are you talking about?" I ask dubiously.

Chad takes my hands in his. "Go over there and apologize to her like she requested. Tell her about the pregnancy and that you want her to be a part of our child's life. And then tell her about the computer searches you found, and say you're scared. Ask her if she ever suspected Shana's death wasn't an accident. All the while you'll be recording the conversation."

I snatch my hands away. "No! Absolutely not. You can't ask me to do that."

"I'm not going to allow you to put my sister in danger," Robin interjects, a firm twist to her lips.

"She won't be in any real danger," Chad says. "I'll slip in the back door and hide in the house and listen in. We're just trying to get Mom to slip up and say something about Shana's death that we can take to the police."

"And what if she turns on Eva—pulls out a knife and stabs her, or something?" Robin asks.

"She's not going to leave a trail of bloody bodies. She's too devious for that."

"You're assuming she hasn't lost the plot yet," I say. "She's completely unhinged. There's no telling what she'll do."

"I wouldn't call her unhinged. She's calculating," Chad says. "Which is why she's got away with everything so far, and got everybody believing she's the injured party. We need the truth to come out, and the only way to do that is to set her up."

"Brandy's never going to agree to this," I say, sensing my defenses breaking down.

"She will if you persuade her," Chad says, a pleading look in his eyes. "The only way we can put an end to this nightmare is to trap Mom into incriminating herself. Do you really want to raise our child constantly having to look over our shoulders, wondering what Mom's next move will be?"

Robin fires Chad a sharp look. "Where are you going to be?"

"In the mudroom. I can hear everything that goes on in the kitchen from there."

Robin turns to me. "It's up to you. You might be able to get something that will force the police to investigate Shana's death."

I hesitate, chewing on the inside of my cheek. It's the last thing I want to do. The idea of coming face-to-face with Laura again, let alone having a conversation with her while pretending to grovel, nauseates me more than being pregnant ever has. But the possibility of having her investigated for capital murder is very alluring.

If I do nothing, she'll be right back at her campaign of sabotage in no time. Besides, there's something in me that wants to entrap her, for Shana's sake, if nothing else.

Laura asked me in her letter to finish what she started and prove that Chad killed Shana.

But maybe I can prove who the real killer is.

48

"What if Brandy double crosses us?" I ask Chad as we drive to her house on Saturday morning. "She might warn your mother what we're up to."

Chad gives a tight-lipped grimace. "She won't betray us. Worst case scenario, she refuses to have anything to do with our plan. But I'm guessing she'll go along with it."

"How do you feel about seeing your mother again after everything that's happened?" I ask, throwing Chad a curious look.

He gives an indifferent shrug. "She blew off our wedding, and she did everything she could to drive us apart. I don't feel anything for her anymore."

I swallow the lump in my throat. It sounds like a harsh thing to say about a parent, even though it's fully justified. I only hope he doesn't cave once he sees his mother again—*if* he sees her again. She's played so many games already that I'm not holding my breath she'll show up at her house on Sunday.

Brandy opens the door to us dressed in black leggings

and a sleeveless yoga top. "Sorry I'm all sweaty," she says. "I came straight from class." She leads us through to the kitchen and pulls open the refrigerator door. "I was about to make a blueberry smoothie. Would you guys like one?"

"Just some water for me, thanks," I say.

"Water for me too," Chad adds.

The whirr of the blender kills our conversation for a moment or two. Brandy joins us at the table and swallows a mouthful of her smoothie. "Yum! I needed that. So are you two here to talk about names? I've been making a list."

I exchange a fleeting look with Chad before answering. "This has nothing to do with the baby. We're here about your mom. I ended up telling Chad everything. He thinks it's possible that your mother might have killed Shana. So we've come up with a plan to see if we can get her to say something to incriminate herself."

Brandy listens intently to our scheme, her face knotting with anxiety when Chad explains that I will be the bait.

"It's risky," she says. "Eva and I already came up with a safer plan. I was going to pretend I'd had a falling out with you, and wanted to help her punish you."

"That's a long shot," Chad says. "The likelihood that she's going to take you into her confidence is slim to none. She's not that stupid. But she is greedy. If Eva confides in her that she's scared of me after discovering my search history, she might think her plan to drive us apart has succeeded."

"I suppose it might work," Brandy says, wrinkling her brow. "It makes sense why Eva would go to her with her suspicions about Chad. After all, Mom said in the letter that she was your ally and wanted to protect you. But I still think I should talk to her first and see if I can get her to confess to me."

Chad gives a reluctant nod. "Okay. Go over there

tomorrow like you planned, then text us when you're done. If you don't get anything out of her, we'll move to Plan B."

"I really wish now I'd kept that letter," I say. "We could have used it as evidence."

"If this goes well, we'll have all the evidence we need," Chad says grimly. His eyes skirt between the two of us. "So, it's a go then? We're all agreed?"

Brandy nods. "I'm in."

"Me too," I say, taking a shaky breath.

I can't help feeling as though I've just signed my death warrant.

49

I toss and turn most of the night, dreading the dawn of the following day and all it entails. For a short while, I almost believed that Laura was dead and I would never have to face my nemesis again. I should have known better. She's far too clever and calculating to die at anyone else's hands.

As I stare at the ceiling, I keep going over our plan in my head. Something is bothering me, but I can't put my finger on it—something beyond the fact that I'm offering myself up as a sacrificial lamb to a vindictive woman who would like nothing more than to help me exit this life before my time.

My eyes are puffy and shadowed when I finally roll out of bed and drag myself into the bathroom. I look haunted when I should be blooming at this time in my life. Is there nothing Laura can't steal from me? I take a quick shower, then stumble downstairs and make myself a strong coffee. I was relieved to get out of bed after such a long, restless night, but it's almost harder now that I'm up and the waiting game has begun.

Chad joins me in the kitchen a few minutes later. He yawns loudly and stretches his arms above his head. "I slept like a rock. How about you?"

I fire him an indignant look. "Like I was dodging hailstones all night long."

His brows shoot up. "Is that a pregnancy thing?"

"No, you dork. It simply means my thoughts were racing around my brain all night. I barely got any rest."

A concerned expression settles on his face. "Are you worried about going over to Mom's? You don't have to do this if you don't want to."

"I don't want to, but I have to," I say. "We can't live like this. We have to get your mother out of our lives, one way or another."

Chad frowns. "Now you're beginning to sound like her."

I roll my eyes. "I'm not suggesting we give her a taste of her own medicine. I'd settle for seeing her locked up for the next twenty years."

Chad reaches out and closes a hand over mine. "I'm going to do everything in my power to make sure that happens."

His eyes glaze over for a moment, and I know he's thinking about Shana. But there's nothing he can do for her now, other than try to stop the same thing from happening to me.

"Do you want some eggs and toast?" I ask, getting to my feet. "I'm not that hungry, but we should eat something. Brandy could call any time, and we need to be ready to go."

"Sounds great," Chad says. "I'm going to take a quick shower while you whip up breakfast."

I pull out a pan and set it on the stove just as my phone chirps. Glancing down at it, I see a message from Brandy.

Mom never came home.

50

In a fit of rage I reach for the frying pan and slam it down on the metal grate on the stove top. As usual, Laura is calling the shots, jerking us around like we're mute beasts with rings in our noses. We all jump to attention when she's coming to town, alter our plans, then accept the fact that we've been stood up once again.

I reach for my phone and call Brandy. "What's going on? Have you talked to her?"

"I texted her. She won't answer her phone. She messaged back that she's postponed her return for another week. I've had it with her. I'm sorry, Eva, but I don't want to have anything more to do with her."

I grip the phone a little tighter in the palm of my hand. I understand Brandy's sentiment in the heat of the moment, but we're going to need all of us to work together if we're going to get to the truth of who was behind those ominous decision computer searches, and what really happened to Shana.

"I get that you're frustrated with her," I say. "We all are.

But let's not make any rash decisions. I'll talk it over with Chad and see what he wants to do."

Brandy releases a heavy breath. "Fine. But we can't keep going like this. We all have lives to lead. I canceled my plans for this weekend to accommodate her. I'm not doing it again."

"Agreed. From here on out, we set the terms. I'll call you back once Chad gets out of the shower and I've had a chance to talk to him."

When he walks back into the kitchen, I'm slumped in a chair at the table glaring out the window. He looks around the room, a puzzled expression on his face when he spots the empty pan sitting askew on the grate. "Did you change your mind about the eggs?" he asks. "I can make them if you feel nauseous."

I flap a hand in his direction. "I just talked to Brandy. Guess who never showed up."

His face crumples with disappointment. He sinks down at the table and squeezes his jaw. "We've got to rethink this. She's controlling our lives. Who knows how long this extended vacation of hers will go on?"

"You might have to pay her lawyer a visit," I say. "Surely this is illegal—disappearing on your family and claiming that your son killed you."

Chad shrugs. "Hearsay, now that you destroyed the letter."

I groan. "Don't remind me. I don't know what I was thinking. It was a spur-of-the-moment thing—an emotional outburst."

"I don't think speaking with her lawyer is going to help anything," Chad says.

"It's worth a try," I say. "He didn't know anything about

the contents of the letter, but that doesn't mean to say he doesn't know where your mother is."

Chad reaches for his phone. "I'll call Brandy and run it by her."

He hangs up after she agrees to accompany him, then calls Sterling and Hackett and makes an appointment with Roger Hackett for the following morning.

Chad and I spend the rest of the day mowing the lawn and taking care of some outdoor chores. I turn in early, exhausted from lack of sleep. Just as I'm about to drift off, I realize what it is that's been bothering me. It's something Brandy told me about her mother: *she said in the letter that she was your ally and that she only wanted to protect you.*

The problem is I never told Brandy that, and I never showed her the letter.

51

I sit bolt upright in bed, electrical impulses firing in all directions in my brain. A sheen of sweat breaks out on the back of my neck. Did Brandy really say that, or did I imagine it? Maybe I did tell her about it and I simply forgot. Except I distinctly remember leaving out that part of the letter because it put Laura in a favorable light to say she was my ally and wanted to protect me—petty on my part, I know. But I was resentful of her after all the hateful things she'd done.

Chad is snoring next to me, so I throw the covers aside and slip quietly out of bed. I pad downstairs to the family room and curl up on the couch with a blanket. I need to think this through and figure out what it means. Did Brandy see the letter that Laura wrote? Did she know about it all along—is she in on everything? My chest feels like it's on fire. She might even have helped Laura write the letter.

Then another thought strikes me. Could Brandy have written it pretending it was from Laura? That would mean she's been sending all those messages from her all along. But why? What's in it for her? She doesn't stand to inherit anything, unless ... my brain goes into scramble mode as it hits me. Brandy stands to inherit everything if her mother is dead, and I'm dead, and Chad's dead, and our baby's dead. Am I crazy for even thinking this way? She was a bridesmaid at my wedding, she's been nothing but supportive from the very beginning—even defending me against her mother's attacks. She adores Chad, and he adores her. I must have got the wrong end of the stick. I squeeze my head between my hands. This can't be true. It doesn't make any sense. She can't be intending to kill her entire family. There's something I'm missing.

I'm about to dial Robin's number when I think better of it. Knowing her, she'll go straight over to Brandy's house and confront her, just like she came right out and asked Chad if he'd killed his mother. But that's not the right way to handle this. I'm never going to get to the bottom of anything unless I come up with a better idea than bold and brash confrontation. My head begins to nod on my chest as the weariness of stress and pregnancy takes over.

When I wake, the sun is spreading an orange glow over the horizon. I stretch my legs out and slowly get to my feet. My mouth feels parched, and I make my way into the kitchen to get something to drink. Sinking down at the table, I cradle my glass of water, my eyes glazing over as I stare through the back window.

I startle almost out of my skin when Chad walks in.

"You look contemplative," he says.

I give a benign smile. I can't tell him what I'm really thinking. He'll be devastated. He might even get angry with me for daring to cast aspersions on Brandy. I need evidence to back it up before I share my suspicions with him.

"Did you eat yet?" Chad asks, rummaging through the cereal boxes in the pantry.

"I'm not hungry." I clear my throat. "There's something I wanted to ask you. Do you think Brandy holds it against you that you're having a child and she's unable to?"

He throws me a stricken look. "No. But I hold it against myself. It's all my fault."

52

I gape at Chad in bewilderment. "What are you talking about?"

He slumps down in a chair and lets his head sink into his hands. "It was a childhood accident that left her infertile. She fell out of her upstairs bedroom window—broke her pelvis in two places and suffered extensive internal injuries."

"That's awful," I say, my heart racing as I digest this new information. Why am I only learning about this now? Did Chad push her or something?

"That must have been terrifying for her," I say. "How old was she at the time?"

"She'd just turned eleven."

For a moment, I'm taken aback. For some reason, I pictured this happening when they were toddlers and didn't know any better. "How on earth did she manage to fall out of the window?" I ask.

"It was my fault," Chad says. "I was the one who came up with the idea. I was always dreaming up crazy pranks as a kid, and I egged her on to do it. We tied a bunch of sheets together like they do in the movies, thinking we could slide down into the garden and sneak out of the house. Stupid, I know. We learned the hard way that movies have stunt doubles." He heaves out a breath before continuing.

"Brandy was a year older so I insisted she go first. It was awful. I can still hear the sound of that sheet shredding as she tumbled to the ground. She didn't even remember it happening. She was unconscious when the ambulance arrived."

I shudder. "Poor thing. That's sounds really traumatic."

Chad gives a melancholic nod. "It was a grueling recovery. She was out of school for months, and she underwent a lot of physical therapy. I didn't understand the long-term repercussions of her injuries at the time, but it's really hitting home now that I'm going to be a father."

I walk over to him and wrap my arms around him. "You have to forgive yourself. You were only a kid at the time."

"Old enough to know better," he says with a grunt.

Old enough to know better. I turn the thought over in my head. Is that what Brandy thinks too? She might have secretly been holding a grudge against Chad all these years. Is she out to destroy his life in return? Is Laura in on it? They could have schemed together to get rid of Shana. Were they hoping to benefit from Chad's life insurance policy after they finished him off too? If that's the case, I must have been a thorn in their side when I came along. No wonder Laura did everything in her power to scare me off.

It's on the tip of my tongue to spill my guts to Chad, but if I'm wrong he'll never forgive me for thinking the worst of Brandy. Without any evidence, I risk souring my relationship with my husband by maligning his sister. I need to do some investigation first. Brandy gave me the code to get into her house to water her plants while she was gone at a library convention a few months back. I'll let myself in while she's at work and snoop around a bit—see what I can find.

Maybe it's wishful thinking on my part, but I'm willing to believe anybody's a killer but my husband.

53

I call in sick to work but get dressed as usual so I don't arouse Chad's suspicions. He always leaves before me so he'll be none the wiser. I've gone over this again and again in my head, and I can't see any other way forward. Brandy knew about the part of the letter I didn't tell her about. Either my mother-in-law is still alive—possibly living at Brandy's house—and was working with her all along, or Brandy has killed her. Neither scenario gives me a warm and fuzzy feeling. Despite how I feel about Laura, she's still Chad's mother, and the idea of her adoptive daughter killing her is terrifying.

"Do you have a busy day lined up, honey?" Chad asks, as he fills his travel mug with coffee.

I swallow the guilt lodged in my throat. "It shouldn't be too bad. We don't have any court dates to prepare for tomorrow. What do you want to do for dinner?"

"How about I pick up something from that new Thai restaurant we wanted to try?" Chad suggests, slinging his briefcase over his shoulder.

I flash him a vacant smile. "Sounds great."

"Try not to work late," he says, as he pulls me in for a kiss. "Maybe we can watch a movie later."

I see him off, then sink back down at the kitchen table, my legs trembling beneath me. Lying to my husband is the hardest part of this whole thing, even though he hasn't been totally honest with me either. I pull up the location app on my phone and track his movements for the next few minutes to make sure he's actually on his way to work. Maybe it's paranoia, but I'm not sure if I can trust anyone in the Turner family anymore. I've got an hour to kill before I can head to Brandy's house. The library doesn't open until 10:00 a.m., but Brandy starts work at eight—checking in and shelving books in preparation for the day. I want to get to her house as early as possible to get this over with. I can't live in limbo any longer. I need to know if my mother-in-law is dead or alive, and I'm convinced the answer lies in Brandy's house.

I pace back-and-forth across the kitchen floor, drinking way too much caffeine to pass the time. I'm tempted to call Brandy on some pretext or other to make sure she's at work, but my brain seems to have turned to mush and I can't come up with anything that sounds even remotely plausible.

When enough time has passed, I grab my purse and hurry out to my car. I just want to get this over with. Maybe I'm completely off base, or maybe I won't find any evidence one way or another, but I have to do something other than sit and wonder.

Twenty minutes later, I pull up outside her house. I sit in my car for several minutes watching the place for any sign of movement inside. A couple of people stroll by walking their dogs, and I keep my head ducked down. I don't want to attract any attention, or allow anyone the opportunity to get a good look at my face in the event that things go sideways.

Once I've managed to calm my nerves sufficiently, I exit my car and make my way up to the front door. For a brief moment, I consider abandoning the plan entirely and going back home with my tail between my legs. But I'll never be able to rest easy knowing I was this close to getting the answers I so desperately need.

I grit my teeth and punch the four-digit number into the keypad. The lock whirrs acceptance of the code, and I depress the handle and step inside the hallway. Closing the door behind me, I lean back against it and scrunch my eyes shut.

My heart feels like it's worked its way halfway up my throat. I'm afraid to open my eyes, fearful Laura's looming over me, knife in hand.

54

Taking it as a good sign that I haven't been stabbed in the heart, I pluck up the courage to open my eyes. If Laura is here, and alive, it's odd that she didn't hear the door opening and come to investigate.

I take a few calming breaths, trying to decide where to start in my search for answers. The problem is, I don't even know what I'm looking for. I head into the kitchen and walk over to the small office area where Brandy keeps her computer. I try a couple of code combinations, including her birthday, to no avail. Abandoning the idea of browsing her computer, I open her desk drawer instead. I rummage through the abandoned pieces of paper—grocery lists, receipts, coupons—but find nothing of interest.

I slam the drawer shut and make my way into the family room next. Brandy is an avid reader and her bookshelves are stacked from top to bottom with everything from biographies, to novels, to self-help. Her shelves are beautifully organized and color-coded. I glance at a few of the spines but don't find anything incriminating—nothing like *Confessions of a Serial Killer*. I let out a weary sigh. This is a lost cause. How am I going to find something when I don't even know what it is I'm looking for?

I spot some photo albums on the bottom shelf and pull one out to take a closer look. I quickly lose myself in the pictures, taking a walk through Brandy and Chad's childhood. I flinch when I come to several photos of Brandy lying in a hospital bed, eyes shut, tubes going into her in multiple locations. Her entire body appears to be in a cast. Chad wasn't exaggerating about the extent of her injuries. She's lucky to be alive.

She couldn't have known as an eleven-year-old child what the ramifications of her accident would be. But as she grew into adulthood, she might have begun to resent Chad for what he'd done to her, intentional or not. I flick through several more photo albums and happen on some photos of Chad and Shana's wedding. It's hard not to be jealous of the way they're looking at each other with such love in their eyes. No one could look at those photos and think that Chad would ever kill his wife. But then again, I've watched enough true crime specials to know it happens.

I snap the album shut, suddenly aware that I'm wasting time. Photos don't prove or disprove anything. I need hard evidence. I get to my feet and make my way to the staircase. If Brandy's hiding any secrets, they must be in her bedroom. I listen for a minute or two, to make sure no one's walking around in the house, then slowly pad upstairs. I hesitate outside the guest bedroom. The door is closed and I can't help wondering if Laura might be staying here. My heart hammers a death knell as I slowly depress the door handle. Everything in me wants to cut and run, but I need to see this through. I push the door open, my eyes darting around the empty room. The bed is immaculate and there's no evidence that anyone's stayed here recently—no clothes or suitcase in sight.

I let out a breath and retreat from the room, pulling the door closed behind me. Mustering my courage, I make my way to Brandy's bedroom next. Gingerly, I squeeze the handle and push the door open, fully prepared to fight for my life if need be.

An eerie silence descends over me. My eyes dart around the room and settle on the most disturbing sight I could possibly have imagined.

55

I retreat a couple of steps, my chest heaving up and down as I stare in shock at the white bassinet with the sleeping infant next to Brandy's bed. My mind floods with confusion. There's so much wrong with this situation that I almost turn and flee the house. But I can't leave this baby alone. Could Laura be looking after it while Brandy's at work? But where is she? Surely she wouldn't have stepped out, even for a few minutes, and left such a young child unattended. My heart slugs against my chest. This is criminal. I have to call the police, or notify Child Protective Services or something. But how am I going to explain what I was doing in Brandy's house to begin with?

My heart is halfway up my throat as I tiptoe quietly across the room and peer into the bassinet. The infant is in a deep sleep, sucking a pacifier, its chest rising and falling with each tiny breath. But something isn't adding up. Slowly, I stretch out my fingers and touch its face, then shrink back in horror. It's not a living baby at all—it's a silicone doll. I take a minute to gather my wits, then reach for it to examine it more closely. I gasp in disbelief when its eyes pop open and it coos at me. It weighs as much as an infant and I can feel its heartbeat in my hands. I've never seen anything more lifelike and unsettling at the same time. I turn the doll over and check the battery compartment on the back. I've heard about these reborn dolls before. They're supposedly therapeutic for people who've experienced the loss of an infant, but nothing about it appeals to me. It's creepy—like handling a dead child. Maybe it works for dementia patients, but there's something macabre about fully functioning adults pretending their dolls are alive.

I place the doll back in the bassinet, and try to position its floppy body in the same spot that I found it. I'm sick to my stomach trying to figure out what this means. I was worried about how Brandy was going to cope once my baby is born, but this is worse than anything I imagined. Just how disturbed is she? On impulse, I pull out my phone and take a picture.

I take a few calming breaths and try to think through my next steps. Freaky doll aside, I still need to search Brandy's bedroom for any evidence that she was involved in Shana's death—or might be involved in helping plan my own demise. I turn my attention to the closet and begin by lifting down the plastic containers from the shelf above the rail and rummaging through them. They're mostly full of receipts, old birthday cards, ticket stubs, and miscellaneous items. At the back of the closet on the floor, I find a plastic file box and flip open the lid. It's jammed to the hilt with documents. I glance at the tabs and realize with a jolt that they're folders full of medical records.

I hesitate for only a moment before digging through them. I'm sure I'm breaking every law on the books by looking at my sister-in-law's medical records, but this could be the key to everything. I don't know what to believe anymore—I'm not even sure if she's really infertile. With shaking fingers, I pull out the first folder and start flicking through it. My heart breaks for her as I see page after page documenting the multiple surgeries she was forced to injure over the years—all stemming from the accident.

I continue browsing through the files until I come to a surgery from six years ago. Tears prick at my eyes. Brandy had a hysterectomy. She wasn't lying about her infertility, but it's unclear if it was the accident that caused it. Is she conning Chad into believing it's his fault so she can manipulate him? A pang of guilt goes through me when I think about how easily I got pregnant. It must be devastating for her to know she'll never carry her own child. I continue browsing through her medical history until I happen upon a particularly thick file at the back of the box. As I begin reading, the ball of fear in my throat swells until I can scarcely breathe.

The patient presents with a complex psychiatric history, with concerns primarily surrounding symptoms of psychosis stemming from an inability to accept her infertility. Currently experiencing paranoid delusions and auditory hallucinations that instruct violent behavior. These episodes are often followed by significant depressive episodes, where the patient experiences persistent low mood, feelings of worthlessness, and thoughts of self-harm. The patient is highly impulsive, and without appropriate intervention, there is a substantial risk of harm to others, especially in situations of perceived threat or hostility.

As the patient is at risk for violent behavior and requires close supervision in a secure setting, inpatient hospitalization is recommended.

56

My throat feels like it's closing over. Why didn't Chad ever warn me that Brandy suffered from major mental health issues? I get that she might have wanted to keep the information private, but I'm his wife, after all. I interacted with her on a regular basis—I was often alone with her. And her diagnosis was dire—*violent behavior, risk of harm to others.* Granted, the report I found was from years ago, but who's to say if she's any better now? Maybe she's just better at masking her issues. And what does the doll say about her current state of mind? Chad likely knows nothing about it.

I slump down on the floor and begin skimming through the detailed reports, trying to glean more information about Brandy's mental health. There are discharge papers from a facility called Ascend Behavioral Health, but I can't find any confirmation that she's been cured—if it's even possible to be cured of psychosis. I frantically leaf through the rest of the medical paperwork, but there's nothing in there to allay my fears.

A rivulet of sweat trickles down the back of my neck. There must be a reason Chad hid all this from me. Was he afraid I would reject him—that I wouldn't want my children to have a mentally unstable aunt and grandmother in their lives? Or is there a more nefarious reason, as Robin suggested? All my fears come crashing down on me at once. Just when I'd decided that I could trust my husband, I'm doubting him again. I can't keep riding this roller coaster. I need this to come to an end, one way or another.

Mustering my courage, I set about continuing my search for answers. I flip through several more pages of medical records until I find myself staring at an oncology report. *High-grade serous carcinoma—ovarian cancer.* I let the information sit in my mind for a moment. So it wasn't the accident that caused Brandy's infertility after all. She's been holding a pernicious lie over Chad's head. In return he's been faithful to keep her mental health history from being exposed—putting me at risk in the process. I'm not sure what that says about him or his priorities. It's disheartening to know he's a weaker man than I thought.

I lay out what I deem to be the most important medical files and snap a few pictures with my phone, then tidy them up and slip them back into the file box. With renewed determination, I resume my search at the back of Brandy's closet. I spot a plastic tote full of Ziplocs stuffed with warranties and instruction booklets for various appliances. At the back of the tote there are several large unmarked Manila envelopes. The first one contains car and home insurance policies. I thumb through them quickly, not wanting to waste any more time than necessary, then come to a sudden stop when I see a life insurance policy at the back. I pull it out and sink down on the floor clutching it in my trembling fingers. It's a copy of the policy taken out on Shana Turner. Several sections are highlighted, including the coverage amount, the accidental death benefit, and the claim process. I can't think of any good reason why Brandy would have a copy of Shana's insurance policy. Was Chad so incapacitated after his wife's death that he needed his family to step in and handle the administrative details? It doesn't sound like the man I know. Does he even know Brandy has this copy?

After snapping a picture, I slide the policy back into the envelope. I throw a quick glance over my shoulder to make sure there are no creepy dolls watching me, then reach for another envelope. I shake the contents out and stare at them in shock. It's an assortment of newspaper clippings on Shana's death. *Fatal injuries sustained from a fall. Jogger dies after plunging from mountain trail. Woman perishes in fall from popular trail.*

I pick an article out at random and begin reading snippets.

Authorities have confirmed the discovery of a woman's body near a rugged section of the Pine Ridge Trail, nearly four months after she was reported missing. The remains, identified as those of twenty-seven-year-old Shana Turner, were found by a group of hikers on Sunday morning near the base of a steep ravine. Turner, an avid jogger and local resident, disappeared without a trace during a morning run in late March of 2022.

"This is not the outcome we were hoping for, but at least we can give her family the closure they deserve," said Sheriff Brian Hayes.

Initial investigations suggest that Turner may have lost her footing while jogging on the trail and fallen several hundred feet before landing in a narrow ravine. Preliminary autopsy reports confirm that the victim suffered fatal injuries to the head and torso. The body was recovered and transported to the county coroner for further examination.

When I come to the end, I suck in a sharp breath. The report is distressing enough, but the handwritten note at the bottom is even more disturbing.

You served your purpose.

57

Blood roars in my ears as I stare in shock at the ominous note. Am I reading too much into it, or is this confirmation of what I feared all along? Was Shana murdered for the money her life insurance policy would pay out? Did Brandy actually kill her sister-in-law—with Laura's help? Terror grips me at the thought. If they did it once, what's to stop them from doing it again? My eyes dart around the room, a feeling of claustrophobia enveloping me. The walls seem to be closing in on me all of a sudden, like I'm sandwiched between the other Turner women and can't escape. I knew they were hiding secrets, but just how many secrets are there? It feels like a bottomless pit. I don't know who knows what, or who was involved, or to what extent. My greatest fear now is that the Turner family is operating in unison. I feel like I'm caught in a web of evil. The level of Chad's involvement is still in question, but there's no doubt that he must have known more than he let on. At a minimum, he knew Brandy was dangerous, and he chose her privacy over Shana's safety. That alone is a despicable betrayal of his marriage.

I turn my attention to the last remaining envelope at the back of the crate. With a mounting sense of dread, I slide out the document inside. It's an amendment to a life insurance policy—Chad's life insurance policy. My heart sinks as I begin to read.

WHEREAS, the undersigned Policyholder wishes to modify the beneficiary designation under the Life Insurance Policy, the following amendment is hereby made:
    New Beneficiary Name: Brandy Turner
    Relationship to Insured: Sister

I CHECK the date and see that the policy was altered a couple of months after Shana's body was discovered. I chew on my lip as I consider the implications. If Brandy was intending to benefit from Chad's death, she had plenty of time to get rid of him over the past couple of years. So why didn't she? Maybe she couldn't bring herself to do it in the end. I twist my lips, dismissing the thought outright. It's more likely she needed to give it some time. It would have looked suspicious if Chad's death had come on the heels of his wife's unfortunate demise. I feel numb as I reread the amendment to the insurance policy. All this time, I thought Laura stood to inherit everything, but it appears I was lied to. Was she lied to as well?

I don't have all the answers I came for, but one thing is abundantly clear—my life is in danger. I need to pack a bag and go to Robin's and figure everything out from there. I hurriedly stuff the document back into the envelope, replace it in the crate and slide the closet door closed. I've seen enough to convince me that Shana Turner didn't slip from that hiking trail, which makes me question the integrity of the beneficiary of her life insurance.

I reach for my purse, then freeze when a voice calls out, "Going somewhere, Eva?"

58

My scream echoes around the room. Brandy is standing in the door frame grinning at me with an unnaturally wide smile, completely at odds with the frigid look in her eyes.

"How did you enjoy your little scavenger hunt in my house?" she purrs. Her tone is deceptively casual, as though we've just bumped into each other in a coffee shop. *Pleasantly poisonous,* I remind myself. I take a small step backward. At only five-foot-four, she's a good three inches shorter than me. Theoretically, I should be able to take her down, but I can't get the forbidding words from the psychiatric report out of my head. *Highly impulsive. Substantial risk of harm to others.* Instinctively, I move my hands over my belly in a protective manner. It's not just myself I have to worry about anymore. I can't afford to be reckless. I need to wait for the right moment to run.

Brandy's eyes travel down to my stomach. "A good mother wouldn't risk her child's future by breaking and entering. I have every right to prosecute you."

"Don't be ridiculous. You gave me the code to your house."

"I didn't give you permission to go through my paperwork and medical records. That's a violation of my privacy."

"Brandy, I can explain. I just—"

She holds up a hand to stop me. "You don't have to explain anything. I know why you came here. What I want to know is what the red flag was that piqued your curiosity about me?"

I give a sheepish shrug. "You mentioned something from your mother's letter that I never told you about. I knew you had to have seen the letter at some point. Either she showed it to you, or you wrote it."

Brandy throws back her head and laughs. "It's always the simplest things that unravel the best laid plans." Her smile vanishes as quickly as it appeared, her gaze swerving in the direction of the bassinet.

I seize on the moment to appeal to her maternal side. "I'm sorry for everything you've gone through, Brandy. I realize it must be especially hard for you now that I'm pregnant."

Ignoring my comment, she walks over to the bassinet and peers into it. "You shouldn't have touched her. I'm her mother."

"I ... uh, sorry," I say, at a loss as to how to respond. It doesn't feel like the right time to point out that she's talking about an inanimate object made of silicone. "What's her name?" I ask.

She scowls at me. "It's none of your business. You shouldn't be here to begin with."

"How did you know I was here?"

She lifts down a stuffed elephant from atop a chest of drawers and waves it at me. "I was watching you on the monitor." She sets the elephant back down and adjusts its position so it's facing the bassinet once more. "A good mother never leaves her child unattended."

I grimace inwardly. Watching her doll through a baby monitor while she's at work is just another sign of how deeply disturbed she is.

"What happened to Laura?" I ask. "Have you been sending those messages all along? Or is she in on this with you?"

Brandy lets out a hard, caustic laugh. "So many questions. I feel like a celebrity granting an interview."

"I deserve some answers. Did you kill Shana?"

"The fall killed her," she replies, her eyes drilling into me like steel.

Judging by the expression on her face, she's not going to admit to anything so I try a different tack. "Does Chad know what you did?"

"What did I do?" she asks in a saccharine tone, cocking her head to one side and blinking at me as though she's irreproachable.

It doesn't appear as if she's willing to answer any of my questions. I'm only wasting time trying to build rapport. I need to figure out a way to get out of here.

"Robin's expecting me," I say. "I have to get going."

Brandy lets out a heavy sigh. "I'm afraid that's not possible."

I square my shoulders and stick out my chin. I can't let her know that I'm scared of her. "What's that supposed to mean? Are you going to kill me too? You won't get away with it."

She gives a long-suffering shake of her head. "I'm not going to kill you, silly." Her eyes drift to the bassinet. "But I am going to need your baby."

59

My heart lurches in my chest, my legs almost buckling beneath me. "You're never getting my baby! You're crazy!"

"So they tell me." Brandy's lips curl into a sardonic smile. "I can live with that. Normal is overrated."

I grip the strap of my purse and break into a run, attempting to charge past her. At the last second, I see her swing something at the side of my head, then a searing pain takes over my senses.

When I come to, I'm tied to the bed and my mouth is firmly duct taped. I try to scream, but it feels like I'm choking, and I'm terrified I'm about to have a panic attack. I thrash around and find myself staring into the bassinet at the doll with no name. A shudder runs through me. Is Brandy planning to replace her doll with my child? I have to get out of this house of horrors.

I have no idea how long I've been lying here, or if anyone has missed me yet. The left side of my head throbs mercilessly. I don't know what Brandy used to whack me with, but I'm pretty sure I saw a flash of metal right before I passed out.

I don't know how she imagines she's going to get away with this. Surely she doesn't think she can keep me tied up here for the duration of my pregnancy without anyone finding out. For a brief moment, I contemplate the prospect of giving birth in this room with only Brandy to assist. The thought terrifies me. I might not survive the ordeal.

I lose all sense of time, and I'm on the verge of drifting off to sleep when I hear the sound of the door opening. Every muscle in my body tenses. There's nothing I can do to protect myself. I'm helpless—completely at this monster's mercy. My only hope is to find a way to reason with her.

Paralyzed with fear, I watch as she walks up to the bassinet and leans over it, stroking the doll inside as she mutters something to it. When she finally turns her attention to me, her expression is set like flint.

"I'm going to remove the duct tape, if you promise not to scream," she says. "If you do start screaming, I'll be obligated to knock you out again, and I won't be so gentle next time." She lifts a pair of menacing-looking, heavy duty pliers off the bedside cabinet and waves them in my face.

I flinch, recoiling in horror, tugging in vain at my restraints.

A smug smile flicks over Brandy's lips. She replaces the pliers on the bedside cabinet, seemingly satisfied by my reaction, then bends over me and rips the duct tape from my lips in one swift movement. My skin stings, but the relief of being able to breathe freely outweighs the pain.

"Brandy, please, untie me," I say. "I need to use the bathroom. I can't lie in this bed any longer. It's extremely uncomfortable to be on my back and it's not good for the baby. I'm seriously dehydrated."

Her forehead creases in irritation. "I'll let you use the bathroom, so long as you don't try anything stupid."

My thoughts gallop in a hundred different directions. I could attempt to overpower her, but she'll probably whack me on the head again with those massive pliers, and I'm still woozy from the first blow. If there's a lock in the bathroom, I could barricade myself inside and smash the window and try to escape. If I had my phone, I could call for help, but there's no sign of my purse anywhere. Presumably, Brandy has taken it and hidden it somewhere in the house.

I lay still as she unties me, then sit up slowly, groaning at the pain radiating out from the side of my head. Gingerly, I feel the dried blood with my fingers. I'll take a good look at the wound in the bathroom and wash it, so it doesn't get infected. I slide off the edge of the bed and get to my feet, wobbling in the process.

Brandy watches me like a hawk, but offers no assistance.

I make my way unsteadily to the bathroom and close the door behind me, grimacing when I see it has no lock. So much for hatching an escape plan from here. I take my time, trying to think of some way out of this nightmare.

It's not long before Brandy's banging on the door. "Hurry up in there!"

"I'm washing the wound on my head to make sure it doesn't get infected," I call back to her.

"You've had long enough!" she says, flinging open the door. She gestures impatiently to me to come out.

I hesitate for only a moment. I have no choice but to obey. She's still clutching those huge pliers that look like they could deliver a death blow.

Under her direction, I trudge back over to the bed and reluctantly allow her to tie me back up.

"I'm thirsty," I say. "I need some water."

She gives a disgruntled sigh and exits the room.

I take the opportunity to test my bonds once more but, if anything, they're tighter than ever.

Brandy returns a few minutes later with a bottle of Diet Coke.

"I can't drink that stuff. I need water, not caffeine."

Brandy gives an indifferent shrug and turns to exit the room.

"Wait!" I cry out, through parched lips. "I'll drink it."

She turns back around, and unscrews the cap.

"Can you untie me so I can sit up properly?" I say. "I don't want to choke."

She scowls. "We don't have time for that." I wince as she supports my head and holds the bottle to my lips. I take a couple of clumsy gulps and some of the sticky liquid trickles down my neck.

"You can't keep me imprisoned here for the entirety of my pregnancy," I say. "People will be looking for me."

"Yes, they will," she agrees with a sickly smile. "But not for the reason you think. They're going to think you killed your mother-in-law."

60

A fist of fear curls around my lungs, squeezing the very breath from me. "Did you ... kill Laura?"

"No, *you* did." She cackles with laughter, then glances down at her red nails, admiring them from multiple angles. "You were always talking about how much you'd like to do her in—more often than not in earshot of everyone. It's not a stretch to think you went through with it, especially after everything she did to you—she really was a witch to you. Some people might not even blame you for taking her out."

"No one's going to believe I killed her," I choke out. My tongue feels as if it's grown thicker in the past few minutes. It seems as though the room is spinning around me, or maybe I'm slurring my words.

"They might when they discover her body in your car," Brandy says.

I gasp, my chest heaving up and down as I try to snatch a ragged breath. I'm fighting a losing battle to stay in the moment. I experience the sensation of falling down an endless shaft as my eyelids drift closed.

. . .

THE NEXT TIME I come to, I'm still tied to the bed, but everything feels different. I'm seeing floaters, but I can't rub my eyes to clear my vision. I scrunch my eyes shut, and wait a moment or two before opening them again. Confusion immediately floods my brain. I blink furiously, turning my head from one side to the other. Nothing about my surroundings looks right. The bassinet is gone. Instead of the peach-toned walls of Brandy's bedroom, I'm looking at knotty pine wood paneling—the kind that's used in old cabins. There's a musty smell in the room, and a draft coming from somewhere. The only decor on the walls is an old hunting scene that hangs askew from a nail. A small desk sits beneath it, covered in dust.

It slowly begins to dawn on me that Brandy must have drugged me and moved me to a different location—someplace remote where no one will think to look for me. The weight in the pit of my stomach grows heavier when I remember what Brandy said about putting Laura's body in my car. The police must be looking for me by now.

My stomach growls, and I try to recall when I last ate. Is there any food in the cabin? Fear blisters over my skin when I realize I might be alone. What if Brandy leaves me tied up for hours at a time—overnight, possibly? The cabin can't be more than then an hour or two from her house, otherwise, she wouldn't be able to go to work—it would arouse suspicion if she didn't go about her business as usual.

My spirits sink even deeper at the prospect of spending the night here. I can tell it's still light out even though the curtains are drawn across the one small window. The only thing about this dreary room that's an improvement on my previous prison environment is the absence of the creepy silicone doll. Brandy must be obsessed with having a baby. How is she planning to pass my child off as her own? A simple DNA test will prove otherwise. I swallow the hard knot in my throat as an even more dire thought occurs to me. The only way she could pull this off is if she disappears with my child. Maybe that's precisely what she's planning to do—live off grid, or even leave the country.

The door suddenly creaks open and Brandy appears carrying a tray. "I thought you might be feeling peckish," she says in a tone so pleasant it throws me off for a minute. Is she slipping in and out of personalities? Is that part of her psychosis? Maybe now would be a good time to try and reason with her.

"Thank you, Brandy. I'm really hungry." I say, attempting a doleful laugh. "Seems like I'm hungry all the time these days."

A flicker of concern crosses her forehead. "I'll make sure you get enough calories throughout the pregnancy."

"Brandy," I say, in a pleading tone. "Let me go home. For my baby's sake, I need to be in a safe place where I can visit my gynecologist for regular check ups. And I want to be with my husband."

She narrows her eyes at me as she sets the tray down on the dusty desk. "Your *husband* owes me. He took away my ability to have children, and now I'm going to take his child from him."

"That's not true. You had ovarian cancer, remember?"

She throws me a look of disgust. "That's irrelevant. My fallopian tubes were severely damaged in the accident. I could never have had a child anyway."

61

"Brandy, let me go, please," I say. "I had nothing to do with your accident. Chad and I both want you in our child's life—as aunt and godmother." It almost kills me to say the words, even though I meant them when I originally told her we wanted her to be involved in every possible way. Back then, it was only my mother-in-law I didn't trust to be anywhere near our baby.

Brandy unties my hands and helps me sit up in the bed, before placing the tray in my lap. I'm tempted to smash it over her head, but my feet are still secured to the bed posts and it would be easy for her to turn the tables on me in half a heartbeat. Besides, I need to keep up my strength if I'm going to break out of here. I'm guessing we're a ways from civilization, so I need to be in good enough shape to hike out of here to the main road. The smartest thing I can do right now is work on gaining Brandy's trust.

I dig into the sandwich and munch through half of it with Brandy eyeballing me the entire time. Apparently, she wants to make sure I eat enough to keep my baby healthy. I eye the water bottle she brought me with suspicion. "You're not planning on drugging me again, are you?"

She juts out her bottom lip. "No need. I had to make you compliant to make the transportation process a little easier. You can scream your heart out here and no one's going to hear you."

I'm not sure I believe her that she hasn't tampered with the water, but I'm so dehydrated I don't even care if it's dosed with sedatives. Tentatively, I unscrew the cap on the bottle and take a generous sip. I gulp down several more mouthfuls, then pick my sandwich back up. "Did you kill your mother?" I ask.

Brandy twists her lips. "We've already discussed this, but maybe your memory's a little foggy. You killed her."

"Let me rephrase my question," I say. "Is your mother really dead?"

Brandy cocks her head to one side and studies me for a moment. "Bet that would make you feel good, knowing she was no longer around to torture you."

I blink and avert my eyes. I can't lie and say I'd be completely devastated if I never saw Laura again, but this is a horrific way for our strained relationship to end. I can only imagine how shattered Chad is going to be.

I rack my brain for a way to pose a question that will hopefully draw out an answer instead of making Brandy put up a wall. "Explain to me why your mother had to die."

Brandy leans back against the desk and gives an approving nod. "Now that is a good question. You never did get what she was trying to tell you, did you?"

I let out a humph. "That I was a worthless wife, not good enough for her son, not fit enough, not pretty enough, not a pianist—I really got marked down on that one."

Brandy smirks. "She was trying to drive you away—she didn't want you to die like Shana."

62

Brandy's words swirl around in my brain as I try to make sense of them.

"What ... what do you mean?" I ask.

"Exactly what I said. I'll leave you to think on it for a bit," she replies, reaching for the tray.

I grab hold of her wrist and squeeze hard. "You're my sister-in-law. I thought we had a real friendship. The least you can do is tell me the truth."

"The truth is whatever you want it to be," Brandy growls, yanking her wrist free. She slams the tray down on the desk and proceeds to tie me up again. I comply, knowing I need to wait for the right opportunity before making an ill thought-out move. I'm not in imminent danger as long as I have what Brandy wants—the baby that's growing inside me. After the birth, all bets are off. But I intend to be long gone before that day arrives.

"When are you coming back?" I ask, fearful that she might be going to drive back to our house and leave me alone.

"When I feel like it," she retorts.

"What if I need to use the bathroom?"

She reaches into her pocket and sets a small bell next to my hands. "Ring this for maid service." She sneers as she turns on her heel and marches out of the room.

I sink back on the scratchy pillow, grateful to rest my aching head. I keep trying to come up with some kind of escape plan, but my options are severely limited. At some point, I drift off to sleep and wake after darkness has descended. My bladder is full and I fumble around for the bell and ring it. Minutes go by with no sign of Brandy, and I start to panic. I pick up the bell again and ring it as loudly as I can.

Eventually, the door opens and Brandy enters the room. She's dressed in fluffy green tartan pajamas which is oddly comforting. I take it as a sign that she's not going to leave me here in the cabin alone tonight.

"I need to use the bathroom," I say.

She gives a curt nod and proceeds to untie my hands. To my relief, I don't see any sign of the menacing looking pliers she used to knock me out with earlier. She pulls a zip tie from her pocket and secures it on my ankles before untying the rope securing me to the bed.

"You'll have to crawl but you're free to use the bathroom on your own. I'm not going to get up and down all night catering to you. The door's locked so there's no way out, and you can't run far with your feet ziptied together anyway, so just behave and get some rest." She throws me a loaded look. "It's good for the baby."

My heart skips a beat as I consider this tiny step in the direction of freedom. I try not to look elated as I shuffle inch by inch toward the bathroom, leaning on the walls for support. There's no way I'm crawling through the filth on the floor like a worm at her feet. A moment later, I hear the bedroom door slam shut and the key turn in the lock. I stumble into the bathroom and do a quick assessment of my surroundings. The only way out is through a tiny transom window at the top of the shower. Even if I positioned the desk below it and stood on it, the window is far too small for an average adult to crawl through. I flush the toilet and wash my hands at the sink, staring at my sunken eyes in the mirror. This isn't exactly the pregnancy bloom I was hoping for.

I hobble back out to the bedroom and over to the small curtained window to the left of the bed. To my dismay, I discover bars outside. Either someone was intent on bear-proofing this cabin, or they were planning to use it to imprison someone. I have a feeling I know where the truth lies. Fear ripples through me.

I can't believe this nightmare is happening. My sister-in-law has morphed into a monster right before my eyes. I frown, thinking over what she said about Laura. *She was trying to drive you away. She didn't want you to die like Shana.*

Is it possible my mother-in-law was trying to save me all along?

63

I spend the night going over all my interactions with Laura as best I can recall. It always seemed in the moment that everything she was doing was purely out of spite—to demean me, or put me down, because she didn't think I was good enough for her son. In hindsight, she did an excellent job of trying to scare me off, if that was her real intention. In fact, if it hadn't been for Brandy's warmth and kindness, she might well have succeeded. I felt supported by my sister-in-law from the very beginning, and of course I loved Chad—I still do. Which is why I've been avoiding thinking too much about his role in all of this. Who exactly was Laura trying to save me from?

For now, I'm going to focus all my efforts on hatching a plan to get out of here. It needs to be a solid one. I can't make a half-baked unsuccessful attempt to flee—it will only make Brandy more determined to revert to the inhumane practice of keeping me restrained. Despite the difficulty of walking with my ankles bound together, it's a whole lot better than being tied to the bed. I run my eyes over the space, searching for anything I could possibly use as a weapon, but other than the curtains and the threadbare blanket on the bed, my options are few.

I reach for my water bottle and drain the rest of it. I'm still thirsty, and I know it's important to stay hydrated during pregnancy, but I'm unsure if it's safe to drink from the faucet in the bathroom. I'm guessing the water in the cabin comes from a well so it should be okay—at least I know Brandy can't drug me if I'm drinking it. I might as well refill my bottle now. It's not as if I have anything better to do to pass the time.

Gripping the bottle in one hand, I begin the long laborious process of returning to the bathroom at a snail's pace. The last thing I want to do is trip and injure myself, and further hamper my ability to escape. It would be a whole lot quicker and easier to get down on all fours and crawl, but I can't bring myself around to the idea of dragging myself through the dirt. I may be Brandy's captive, but I can still preserve whatever dignity I have. Once I reach the desk, I stop to rest. My gaze falls on a jagged shard of banding that's come loose on the bottom drawer. I regard it for a moment, weighing its usefulness, but realistically, it's too flimsy to use as a weapon. It would simply snap in half if I tried to stab Brandy with it.

When I finally make it into the bathroom, I sit on the toilet lid for a few minutes to catch my breath. I almost wish I'd brought the blanket from the bed with me so I could take a nap in the bathtub. The thought of shuffling all the way back to the bedroom using minuscule movements that are taxing my muscles and causing cramps in my calves is truly disheartening. I push myself to my feet and make the trek over to the sink trying not to topple in the process. After refilling my bottle, I down half of it, then refill it again. I stare blankly at my face in the dirty mirror. Maybe it's the air of desperation in my eyes, or the cumulative lack of sleep, but I look even more haggard today than I did yesterday.

My eyes sweep over the space once again, hoping by some miracle to find a tool, a nail, or a rusty razor blade— anything that could help me in my bid to escape. But Brandy has left nothing to chance. There's not as much as a washcloth or a bottle of shampoo in sight. She hasn't even left me a towel to dry off with. Does she think I might try to strangle her with it? My gaze flits to the toilet, and a nugget of an idea starts to form. A burst of adrenaline propels me as I shuffle back across the floor. I reach for the toilet tank cover and lift it. Could this be my ticket out of here? It's got enough weight to it to do some real damage. The problem is, it's not the easiest weapon to disguise. It's not as if I can slip it up my sleeve and take Brandy by surprise. I need a plan that will distract her long enough for me to take a swing at her. My lips curve slowly into a smile.

I know exactly what to do.

64

When Brandy returns a few hours later, I'm lying on the bed in a fetal position with the bell next to me.

"Breakfast is served," she chirps, standing in front of me with a tray of scrambled eggs on toast. The tantalizing smell of coffee taunts my nostrils, and I'm half-tempted to delay executing my plan until after breakfast, but reason prevails.

I let out a small groan, pulling my knees closer to my chest. "I'm not hungry," I lie.

Brandy frowns at me. "I thought pregnant women were always hungry. What's the matter?"

"I don't feel well. I have stomach cramps. I need to see a doctor."

The compassion on Brandy's face melts into a sneer. " Sure you do. I see what's going on here. You're not going to fool me. I'll leave this food on the desk in case you change your mind. I'm sure you'll be thankful for it when you get hungry enough to quit your theatrics. My recommendation would be to drink the coffee while it's hot—much more enjoyable that way."

I hear the clatter of the tray being dropped onto the desk, followed by the sound of the door slamming and locking once more. I let out a long fluttering sigh. Step one completed. Step two is going to be resisting temptation. I could scarf that toast and eggs down in two bites right about now, and I don't even want to think about the taste of the hot coffee. I suppose I could take a couple of sips and fill the cup back up with water, but once I start it will be hard to stop.

I wriggle to the edge of the bed and sit up, salivating as I eye the breakfast from afar. It wouldn't do any harm to take a small bite of the eggs—I could move the toast around on the plate to cover it up. My stomach rumbles, and I make the executive decision to allow myself one small mouthful, for the baby's sake, of course. I reach for the bell and slip it into my pocket, then begin the voyage across the room, made even longer by the fact that I'm walking all the way around the wall so I have some support. By the time I reach the breakfast tray, I'm having second thoughts. What if Brandy has tampered with it? I can't risk being knocked out for the rest of the day. I need to set my plan in motion ASAP.

Gingerly, I hunker down next to the desk and tear off the jagged piece of banding from the bottom. After examining it, I pocket it and straighten back up. It's not great, but it might do the job I have in mind. It takes all my self control to leave the tray of food untouched and keep moving in the direction of the bathroom.

Once inside, I take a few minutes to rest, then reach for the shard in my pocket. I'm not good with blood at the best of times, so I'm praying I don't pass out as I begin the process of trying to saw my finger open. The shard is not as sharp as I thought it was going to be, and I'm not as coura- geous as I'd hoped. It's a tentative effort at best. I can't help wishing I had a pocket knife. At least then I could do some damage in one swift move—less traumatizing and painful than trying to pick open my skin with this flimsy piece of banding. My skin is already red and raw from the effort, but I'm not fooling myself—I'm still holding back. I grip my teeth and tell myself that if I can't drum up the courage to break my skin, then I don't deserve to walk out of here. I count to three, then stab the shard with all my strength into the inside of my pinky finger. Finally, a pinprick of blood appears. I hack at the wound until it starts bleeding more heavily, then quickly smear the blood on my right leg, doing my best to make it look like it trickled down. I repeat the process until there's enough blood on my leg to raise an alarm.

Satisfied with the job I've done, I fish the bell from my pocket and ring it.

65

Minutes go by and there's still no sign of Brandy coming to my aid. I keep ringing the bell, and hacking at the wound on my finger to make sure there's a fresh trickle of blood running down my leg. At last, I hear the sound of the bedroom door being unlocked. I lean over the toilet, gripping the tank cover, and let out a long drawn-out moan. I'm almost breathless with terror, and sweat dampens my forehead—which will only add weight to my fabricated predicament. Silently, I count the seconds as Brandy's footsteps approach, quickening in pace as my moaning intensifies.

"What is it? What's wrong?" she asks in a sharp tone, as she bursts through the door. Her eyes drift down to my bare ankle where the trickle of blood that meandered down my leg has made its way.

"I think I'm having a miscarriage," I croak. "I need to get to the hospital."

Brandy's face pales. For the first time, a look of uncertainty crosses her face. "It's probably just spotting. We need to get you back to bed."

"I can't walk that far," I say, in as pitiful a tone as I can conjure up.

"I'll help you," Brandy says.

"I'm dizzy. Can you pass me my water bottle. It's on the sink."

As she turns to reach for it, I flip a switch. Adrenaline surges through my body. In one rapid movement, I lift the toilet tank lid and uncoil my hips, before smashing the lid down on Brandy's head. She drops like a stone at my feet without a word. My hands are shaking violently as I attempt to replace the tank cover. I hope I haven't killed her. That wasn't my intention. I kneel down and check for a pulse. She's alive. But there's no time to waste. I need to get these zip ties off my ankles and make my escape from this cabin.

I pat Brandy's pockets and find the key to the bedroom. Surprisingly, she doesn't have her phone on her. Maybe there's no signal here. I begin another desperate shuffle out of the bathroom and across the bedroom floor to freedom. Halfway there, I abandon any attempt at dignity, drop to my knees and begin to crawl. I'm terrified that, at any minute, she'll jump on me from behind and start strangling me. The thought propels me on until I'm on the other side of the bedroom door. I slam it shut and haul myself to my feet. My fingers are quivering so much I can barely get the key in the lock. Relief floods through my veins when I finally hear a reassuring click.

I lean back against the wall and take stock of my surroundings, allowing my heart to slow its hammering in my chest. I'm standing in a dark, low-ceilinged hallway. Thankfully, the cabin doesn't appear to be very big. I inch my way down the hallway toward the kitchen. My gaze darts over everything at once, tabulating what I need to do—cut myself free, look for a phone, find the car keys, get out of here. I spot a knife block on the counter and hobble over to it, then grab the scissors and cut myself free. Tears of relief prick my eyes. I'll never again take the ability to move freely for granted. I toss the scissors on the counter and look around for Brandy's purse. There's a cast-iron black bear key rack on the wall, but it's empty. I don't see a purse or a tote anywhere. A flight of stairs leads down to what is presumably the basement, but it looks dark and unused. I dart into the adjacent family room and check the shelves, then search behind the cushions on the upholstered tapestry couch. I'm about to give up when I spot a brown leather bag wedged between the loveseat and an end table.

Stomach fluttering with anticipation, I snatch it up and rummage through it. I pull out Brandy's phone in its cheetah print case, but as I suspected, there's no signal. Still, I'll bring it with me and call 911 as soon as I have service. I fish around a little more and locate her car keys in a side pocket. Finding nothing else of value, I toss the purse back on the floor and dash into the kitchen.

I'm about to pull open the back door when a muffled voice cries out "Help! Somebody, please help!"

66

I freeze, every muscle in my body locking in unison. Brandy must have regained consciousness. Everything in me resists the idea of helping her after what she's done to me. No one will hear her yelling in this isolated cabin, as she was only too eager to inform me when she locked me up. I'll call 911 once I'm far enough away to get some service.

"Help! Please!" she calls out again.

I stiffen. That voice didn't come from the bedroom. It drifted up from the basement. My heart begins a rhythmic jackhammering in my chest. Did she escape, or is there someone else in the cabin?

I abandon my plan to exit through the back door, and instead, peer cautiously down the steep dusty staircase, presumably leading to a basement. I hesitate for a moment, then walk over to the knife block and pull out the largest one I can find. Using the light from Brandy's phone, I proceed slowly down the staircase, one step at a time. There's a rickety door at the bottom with a large rusty bolt holding it closed. I peer through a hole in the knotted wood but it's too dark to see anything on the other side. "Who's there?" I call out.

I put my ear to the door and listen. There's a scrabbling sound as though someone's getting to their feet, then footsteps slowly make their way toward me. A fist pounds the inside of the door. "My name is Laura Turner. Please let me out of here!"

I almost keel over from shock, and shoot out a hand to steady myself on the wall. I don't know how to respond, not that I could anyway. My throat is clamped shut. *Laura is alive!* Has Brandy been keeping her prisoner the whole time she was supposedly off traveling?

"Hello? Is anyone there?" Laura calls out, in a thready tone. She sounds nothing like the sharp-tongued woman who spent months lashing out at me in the most hateful ways. Everything in me recoils at the thought of opening the door and seeing her spiteful face again. And then another thought occurs to me. What if this is a trick? Could Laura be in on the whole plan to help Brandy steal my baby? I picture her throwing her head back and howling with laughter at the sight of me, then forcing me at gun point back inside the basement where I'll be forced to remain for the duration of my pregnancy, at which time they'll dispose of me permanently.

I'm caught in a quandary, but I can't in good faith leave Laura locked up in the basement. It's unlikely she's in there voluntarily. Brandy is still locked in the bedroom so, even if Laura tried to tackle me, I could easily overpower her with this knife.

"Laura, it's me, Eva," I reply at length.

I hear her moan softly. "So, she got to you after all. What did she do to you? Are you hurt?"

"No. I'm fine. I'm going to open this door and let you out, but don't try any funny business. I'm armed."

"Thank you. I'll move away from the door so you don't feel threatened."

I wrestle with the bolt for a couple of minutes before managing to slide it across. After pulling open the door, I blink to accustom my eyes to the darkness. A frail figure gets up and walks toward me.

My eyes widen at the gaunt hollowed-out face of my mother-in-law.

67

For a moment, neither of us speak. I'm appalled at Laura's condition. She must have lost thirty pounds since I last saw her, and her skin is ashen gray like she hasn't seen the sun in months. She takes an unsteady step forward, and I shoot out a hand to help her. She hesitates, throwing a fearful look at the knife in my other hand. She's in no condition to pose a threat, so I toss it on the ground and kick it into a corner. "I wasn't sure what to expect," I say with a shrug.

"Where's Brandy?" Laura asks, darting a skittish glance up the stairs.

"She's locked in the bedroom. Let's concentrate on getting out of here and then we can talk."

Navigating the steep staircase with a frail woman who looks like she hasn't seen the light of day in months proves to be no easy feat. It's a painstakingly slow process, but we finally make it up to the kitchen.

"I need some water," Laura says, her breath coming in short snatches as she sinks down on a chair.

I'm anxious to get out of here, but there's a good chance

she'll pass out if she doesn't get something to eat and drink. I fill her a glass of water and hand it to her, then pull open the refrigerator door and scan the contents. I reach for a package of sliced cheese and pass it to her. "Here's something to nibble on while we drive."

When she has satisfied her thirst, I take her by the arm and lead her outside to where Brandy's car is parked in the dirt. After helping her climb in, I slide into the driver's seat. My veins fill with relief at the welcome sound of fuel flooding the engine. I had visions of the car refusing to start, and having to hike for miles out of here, not knowing which direction to walk in, or how long it would take before someone came across us. I throw a quick glance around, but I don't see a house number or a mailbox anywhere. This cabin must be abandoned—either that or Brandy has removed the number so it can't be identified.

"Do you have any idea where we are?" I ask, as I pull out onto a gravel road.

"None, whatsoever." Laura shakes her head despairingly. "Brandy drugged me before she brought me here." She looks across at me. "I take it that's how she got you here too."

I give a grim nod, my fingers instinctively reaching up to feel the knot on the side of my head. "She whacked me on the head and knocked me out. When I came to, I was tied to her bed. She must have put a sedative in the drink she brought me because the next time I woke up I was in the cabin."

"What were you doing at her house in the first place?" Laura asks.

I grimace. "I snuck in to take a look around while she was at work. I suspected she wasn't being honest with me, because she mentioned something that was in the letter you supposedly wrote that I hadn't told her. I realized she must have seen the letter at some point, which meant you either showed it to her, or she wrote it."

Laura rumples her brow. "What letter are you talking about?"

"A letter claiming that you suspected Chad had killed Shana, and that you had done everything you did to scare me off to protect me."

Laura gives a thoughtful nod. "I made the mistake of sharing my suspicions about Chad with Brandy. Sounds like she pretty much wrote down everything I said verbatim. That's when she drugged me and brought me up here. How did she know you were in her house?"

I throw Laura a sideways look. I wonder if she knows about Brandy's doll and her obsession with babies. If she doesn't, she's going to find out soon enough anyway. "She had a baby monitor in her bedroom. She was watching me on it while she was at work."

Laura blinks at me, a baffled look on her face. "Why on earth did she have a baby monitor in her bedroom?"

I let out a regretful sigh before telling her all about the reborn doll and Brandy's plan to keep my baby.

68

I t isn't long before we arrive at an unmarked junction with the option of turning left or right.

"Nothing looks familiar to me. We're just going to have to roll the dice," I say to Laura.

She nods. "I'm guessing either road has to lead us out of here eventually."

"Or else one of them dead ends. I hope we don't run out of gas in the middle of nowhere. Here goes nothing." I turn right and we continue along the gravel road at a maximum speed of twenty miles per hour. We have about half a tank of gas so we're good for now. I should have brought Brandy's purse with me so we'd have some money if we need it.

"So why did Brandy bring you to the cabin?" I ask, bracing myself against the potholes that are shaking me to my bones.

Laura gives a sheepish grin. "I was doing some snooping too. Brandy has always concerned me. I've known since she was a child that something's not quite right with her, but I never suspected she was dangerous. I was more worried that she was depressed or bipolar. She left her purse at my house one day, and I peeked inside and found her diary. It was a few days after your bridal shower, and she had written about it. She was reveling in the reactions to the bloody knife and the ominous note. She said some awful things about you. She resented the fact that you had come along and replaced Shana just when she'd taken care of that problem. I took some pictures of the most incriminating pages.

When she came back to pick up her purse, I confronted her about some of the things she'd written—I even asked her outright if she'd killed Shana. She just laughed. She said I needed to calm down, that she could explain everything. She made us some tea and that's the last thing I remember from that day. She must have put something in my drink. When I woke up, I was in the cabin."

"To say I was shocked when I saw you is an understatement," I say. "Not just the fact that you were in the cabin, but your gaunt appearance. I can't believe how much weight you've lost since I saw you last. Has she been feeding you at all?"

"She brought me one meal a day—packet oatmeal for the most part. I don't know what her end game was—slow starvation, by the looks of things."

"Maybe she didn't know herself. I found her discharge papers from a psychiatric facility called Ascend Behavioral Health," I say. "Her diagnosis said she exhibited symptoms of psychosis and was highly impulsive, and at risk for violent behavior."

Laura turns to me with a confused expression on her face. "What are you talking about? This is the first I've heard about this. I would have known if she'd been committed to a facility. We always kept in touch." She rubs her brow, frowning in concentration. "Although, there was this one time when she was supposedly traveling overseas. She was in remote places with no Wi-Fi for the most part. She touched base with Chad from time to time on some social media app, and he gave me regular updates on her travels. Now I'm wondering if that was all fabricated to keep me in the dark.

I throw her a dubious look. "Are you saying you had no idea your daughter had psychiatric issues?"

"That's exactly what I'm saying." Her face crumples. "It would appear Chad lied to me to cover for her."

My shoulders sag. "He feels guilty about the accident. I think Brandy holds it over him, and uses it as leverage to get whatever she wants."

69

At long last we come to a main junction with a paved road. I roll to a stop and check Brandy's phone, heartened to see one bar. "We must be getting close to civilization," I say. "Once we get a strong enough signal, we can call 911." I hand the phone off to Laura." Keep an eye on it. I'll concentrate on the road."

Minutes later, she lets out a squeal. "I've got three bars."

I give an approving nod. "Try calling 911 now. It's time they picked up Brandy."

THE NEXT FEW hours are an absolute whirlwind as the police take our statements. Laura and Brandy are both admitted to the hospital. The detective in charge informed me that Brandy is being charged with unlawful imprisonment, for starters. I suspect there will be a slew of additional charges coming her way thanks to her detailed diary entries. She might even have documented Shana's murder in an older diary, for all I know. The police will obtain a search warrant and tear her house apart, and confiscate a hoard of evidence, including her reborn doll. They've already begun a forensic analysis of her car.

Chad is waiting for me in the reception area of the station when I'm done giving my statement. He jumps to his feet when he sees me and envelopes me in a hug. "I can't tell you how relieved I am to see you. Are you okay? Did she hurt you?"

"I'm fine," I say. I'm stiff in his arms, unable to reciprocate, after everything I've gone through and everything I've learned about my husband's sister.

"She killed Shana," I say, holding his gaze. "Did you know?"

"No, of course not. And before you ask, I had nothing to do with it."

I don't respond. It seems an odd thing for him to say. I don't know if I believe him, and I don't know how to come to a place of assurance that I can ever trust him again. I still don't know who conducted those searches for ethylene glycol on his computer.

"Let's get out of here," I say. "We can talk back at the house."

We drive home in relative silence. Chad makes a couple of lame attempts to converse with me, but I shut him down. I just need a few minutes to myself to think before we're forced to have a difficult conversation.

The first thing I do when I get home is make myself a chicken sandwich. I gobble it down under Chad's watchful eye. I offered to make him one too, but he insisted he wasn't hungry. When I'm done, I sink back on my chair and let out a satisfied sigh. My husband squirms in his seat, as though waiting on me to hit him with something.

"Why didn't you ever tell me about Brandy's diagnosis?"

N. L. HINKENS

I ask. "I could have been killed—our baby could have been killed."

"It was in the past," he says. "She was treated and cured, so I didn't consider her a threat. I knew you two had grown close, and Brandy said she wanted to tell you about it in her own time and on her own terms. I respected that. I would never in a million years have willingly exposed you and our child to danger."

"But you didn't even report me missing."

"The police won't do anything for the first twenty-four hours. We learned that when we tried to report my mom missing."

"It might have changed things if they'd known I was pregnant."

"Believe me, I tried everything I could to find you," Chad protests. "I was frantic. I called Brandy incessantly, asking if she'd seen you. I even went around to her house and rang the doorbell multiple times. I feel awful about what happened. I'm so sorry."

"So am I. To be honest, I'm not sure how I feel about your role in all of this. I'm going to spend the night at Robin's. I need to decide if we're going to move forward as a couple or not."

70

I pull up outside the apartment that I called home up until a few months ago. Never in my wildest dreams could I have imagined returning under such horrific circumstances. Robin was the first person I called when I left the police station, and she's the only person I trust right now. With her, I can finally rest and let down my defenses, and talk this nightmare through. Maybe she'll have some wise words for me. She's never led me astray so far. I grimace when I remember her advice not to marry into the Turner family to begin with. She had a premonition it wouldn't end well. Too late for that now. The question is whether I should stay in my marriage.

I reach into the back seat for the overnight bag I packed, and head inside the apartment.

Robin gives me a huge hug, which I desperately need, before sitting me down on the couch. She fetches us both a Diet Coke from the kitchen, then pulls out her phone. "I'll order us up something to eat. What do you fancy? Nothing too spicy, I assume."

"Pepperoni pizza sounds good, with a side of Caesar salad."

Robin puts the order in on her phone and curls up on the couch next to me. "What are you going to do?" she asks, sipping her Coke.

"You mean about Chad?"

She nods. "Obviously, your relationship with Brandy has imploded—she's going to be locked up for a long time—but how do you move forward in your marriage knowing that Chad hid her history of mental illness from you?"

I give a helpless shrug. "I don't know. That's why I'm talking to you. I'm hoping to get some clarity on things. I asked him if he knew Brandy had killed Shana. He denied it, but he said something that struck me as strange."

"What's that?" Robin prompts.

"He said 'before you ask, I had nothing to do with it.'"

Robin throws me an alarmed look. "That's disconcerting, to say the least. And it's odd that he never called me to see if you were at my house when you didn't come home last night."

"Maybe he didn't think of it."

Robin rolls her eyes. "I'm your sister. We lived together right up until you got married. It should have been the first call he made. Why would he think you were with Brandy? That's weird."

"I don't know. Maybe I mentioned going over there. My mind's a muddle."

"You're too busy defending him to assess the situation objectively," Robin says, reaching for her can of soda.

"What do you think I should do?"

Robin eyes me over the rim of her can. "Pretend you're going to have the marriage annulled and see how Chad reacts."

I stare at her in bewilderment. "I'm not sure I follow your logic."

"If he married you with the nefarious intention of cashing in a life insurance policy, which you declined to take out, he's hardly going to be devastated if you leave, is he? I think his reaction will be very telling."

When I arrive back at my house the following morning, there's a heavy weight in the pit of my stomach. I'm not looking forward to the conversation I have to have with Chad. It could well be the end of my short-lived marriage.

I find him in the kitchen tapping away on his laptop. When he sees me, he slams the lid closed and shoves it to one side. "Hey! I thought I'd work from home today. I figured we needed to talk."

I make myself a coffee and sit down at the table next to him. "I'm going to make this brief. I've thought long and hard about it, and I've decided to have our marriage annulled."

Chad's expression morphs into one of shock. "Eva, it doesn't have to come to this."

I wave a dismissive hand at him. "It already has. We got married under fraudulent circumstances. You had a psychotic sister who was a danger to herself and others, and you didn't inform me."

"Eva, please. There's nothing I want more than to be a family with you and our unborn child. I realize I've made mistakes, but I'll spend the rest of my life trying to be a better man. I can't be that without you. I know I don't deserve you, but please give me another chance. I'll do whatever it takes to prove myself to you."

I feel numb inside listening to him say all the right

things. At the end of the day, I have to make a choice—leave and build a life without him, or stay and fight for my marriage to a man I love but don't trust.

71

I head upstairs to take a shower, still mulling over what to do. I've sent Chad out to pick us up some breakfast from my favorite bakery on the other side of town—claiming a non-existent pregnancy craving. With him out of the house, it will give me a chance to think in peace, if nothing else.

My discarded clothes from yesterday are still strewn all over the bedroom floor. I'm about to toss them in the laundry basket when I realize that Brandy's phone is still in my sweatshirt pocket. I'd forgotten all about it. I press the power button, but the battery's dead, so I plug it in to charge before I head into the bathroom to wash up. I should probably turn it over to the police, but I'm not going to pass up the opportunity to snoop while I have it in my possession.

I take a lengthy shower, the hot water finally helping to clear my head. I'll talk things through some more with Chad and see what we can work out. If he agrees to go to counseling, we might have a fighting chance. I need him to understand that we can't move forward in our marriage if he's not willing to come clean with me about everything.

I take my time drying my hair and getting dressed, then head back into the bedroom. Brandy's phone has powered up and, to my surprise, she has no password on it. She might have disabled it at the cabin knowing she was the only one with access to it. Curious, I scroll quickly through her emails, but find nothing of interest. I click on her Messages App to see who she's been communicating with. She doesn't appear to have too many friends—a couple of fellow librarians seem to be the extent of it. I read through the messages from Chad, surprised there are none asking about my whereabouts. I check the call log next. A feeling of dread creeps through my bones. Chad told me he had been calling Brandy incessantly, but there isn't a single call from him in the last few days.

I slip the phone into my pocket and snatch up my purse. If I'm not getting the truth from Chad, maybe I can get it from Brandy. I consider leaving a note for Chad, but scrap the idea. He didn't care when I went missing before, so why would he care now? I dart outside to my car and peel out of the driveway en route to the hospital. I'm not sure I'll even be allowed to speak to Brandy, but I'm going to do my best to muscle my way in. Either way, it won't be an entirely wasted trip. I can check up on Laura while I'm there.

As I suspected, there's a police officer stationed outside Brandy's room. Undeterred, I walk briskly up to him. "Can I talk to my sister-in-law for a few minutes? I understand she's conscious."

"Sorry, ma'am. Can't allow that. Security concerns."

I gesture at my belly. "Do I look like a security concern to you? And Brandy's incapacitated with all those tubes going into her." I scrunch up my face as though fighting back tears. "She was going to be my child's godmother."

The officer's expression softens. He casts a quick glance

inside the room. "All right. You can have five minutes with her. Leave your purse outside."

"Thank you," I say, dropping it at his feet and slipping through the door.

I clap a hand to my mouth when I finally see the full extent of what I did to her.

72

Brandy lies silent and still amidst a web of tubes and machines monitoring her vitals. The rhythmic rise and fall of her chest is the only indication that she's even alive. Her face is black and blue down one side, and her left eye is swollen shut. At the sound of my footsteps walking over to her bed, her right eye flickers open. Her empty gaze zeros in on me, her face an expressionless mask. I have no idea if she even recognizes me. I'm stunned into silence, shocked at what I've done to another human being. I guess it's true that a mother will do anything to save her child.

"I'm sorry, Brandy," I begin. "I didn't want to hurt you. I was out of options—I had to do something to get out of there. You weren't thinking straight."

I hear a raspy noise in her throat, and I realize she's trying to talk. I sink down on the stool next to her bed and lean in closer. Maybe she's trying to apologize too.

"I didn't ... kill her," Brandy says in a hoarse whisper.

I furrow my brow. She must mean Laura. "I know. Your mom's safe," I say. "She's here in the hospital."

"Not her." Brandy sucks in a shuddering breath. "Shana."

"You're going to have a hard time proving that after everything you've done," I say. "Your mother found your diary. She took photos of some of the stuff you wrote in it. You were the one who urged Chad to take out the life insurance policies, and you stand to inherit everything if he dies."

Brandy pierces me with a stony one-eyed gaze. "It was ... his idea." She sucks in a couple more breaths. "He said he would go halves with me, and make me the beneficiary of his policy too. All I had to do was ... shove Shana off the trail."

My stomach knots at how calmly she talks about murdering her sister-in-law. How could she possibly have thrown her brother's wife to her death and carried on with her life as usual? "Why would you even consider committing such a heinous crime?"

"Chad threatened to tell everyone that I'd been committed to a psychiatric institution if I didn't do it." Brandy's face contorts as though she's in pain. "I always did everything he told me to, even as a child. At first, I agreed to help him, but I ... I couldn't go through with it. A couple of days later, Shana *conveniently* fell to her death. I knew what he'd done. I threatened to go to the police. Chad told me he would give me half the money to keep quiet, but he never followed through with that. He kept saying it would look suspicious if he were to give it to me too soon. He owed me. That's why I decided to take his baby instead of the money. Mom was getting too close to the truth. She had to be stopped."

I stare at the pathetic figure lying in the bed, wondering how much of her story to believe. I don't want to believe any of it, but the more I think about it, all the pieces are falling into place. Chad was able to manipulate Brandy due to her mental health issues, which he was careful to conceal from me all along.

And now I know why.

73

Ten months later.

My daughter, Avery Marie, is spending the night with her grandmother for the first time. Laura has proven to be the best grandmother I could ever have hoped for. After recovering from her two-month long imprisonment at Brandy's hands, she became my rock throughout the remainder of my pregnancy, and was there alongside Robin at Avery's birth. I'm thankful that my child will have such a loving and involved nana, as she calls her, in her life.

Today, I'm going to make the five-hour drive to visit Chad in prison. I have one final request for him, and after, that I don't intend to set eyes on him ever again. If things go according to plan, my child will never come face-to-face with him. As a result of Brandy's testimony, he's on trial for murder. He denies all wrongdoing—maybe he can convince a jury of that, but he hasn't persuaded me. He's written to me multiple times and requested pictures of our child, but I've ignored all his correspondence to date. He knows I had a girl, but I haven't even told him her name. I'm not convinced his interest in Avery is genuine. He just wants to string me along so he has someone in his miserable life to put money into his commissary account and order stuff for him.

I've scheduled a visit for 3:00 p.m. this afternoon, and studiously read through the visiting guidelines to make sure I don't violate any policies regarding attire and what to bring. After going through the lengthy screening process, I finally enter the visiting room and take my seat at a table. It's a good fifteen minutes later before Chad trudges into the room in his shapeless prison garb. He smiles as he walks toward me, but I don't reciprocate. When he reaches out his arms to hug me, I brush him off and gesture for him to take a seat.

"I'm only here to talk," I say, in a crisp tone.

Chad pulls out the plastic chair opposite me, an injured expression on his face. "Do you have to be so cold?" he whines. "You know I didn't kill Shana. Brandy's a mentally ill pathological liar."

"That's up to the jury to decide. I'm not here to discuss your case. I'm not your lawyer."

"Did you bring me a picture of our daughter?" Chad asks.

"No. It's best you don't get attached. I'm considering giving her up for adoption."

Chad narrows his eyes at me. "I thought you wanted to keep the baby."

I bristle at how he refers to Avery as "the baby," as though she's an object he has no real attachment to. Of course I'm not actually going to give her up for adoption, but maybe it will convince him to quit bugging me for pictures of her.

"I was in love with the idea of a baby," I say, scowling at

him. "But I don't want any part of you in my life. The upside is you won't have to pay child support. You can hold on to more of that money you're so in love with." I pull the divorce paperwork out of an envelope and lay it in front of him, along with a pen.

Chad picks it up and signs in the requisite places. He shoves the documents across the table to me and I slide them back into the envelope, relieved at his lack of resistance. I get to my feet and give him a curt nod. "Goodbye, Chad."

He throws his hands out. "That's it? The visit's over? I did what you wanted and didn't contest the divorce. When am I going to see you again?"

"You're not. We have nothing more to discuss." I turn on my heel and exit the room. I've cut the last remaining cord with Chad Turner, and I won't look back. Everything I do from here on out will be for Avery, and for Avery alone.

74

I climb into my car and start the engine, shaking with relief. My next stop is Silvercrest Meadows, the mental health institution where Brandy is currently housed. It's a couple of hours drive from here so I'll spend the night in a hotel before heading home in the morning. I invited Laura to come with me, but she refuses to have anything more to do with her daughter. I'd prefer not to visit Brandy either, but the manager of the facility said she's been asking for me constantly. Apparently, she's regressed since she was discharged from the hospital. I can't help feeling like it's my fault—like I damaged her brain in my bid to escape. But what choice did she leave me? She was going to kill me after she took my baby. She doesn't know that my child has been born, or what her name is, and she's never set eyes on her, and she never will. It's sad to think that she was once going to be Avery's godmother. After everything that's happened, the thought of sharing details about my daughter with her is just too creepy.

When I finally arrive at the facility, the manager pulls me into his office. "I just want to prepare you," he says, blinking at me from behind his thick glasses. "Brandy's not making a lot of sense at the moment. She's living in a fantasy world."

I frown. "What do you mean?"

The manager gets to his feet. "You'll see."

"She's not a danger, is she?" I ask hesitantly.

He gives an understanding smile. "No, not at all. She's on a high dose of anti-psychotic medication. You'll find her in the communal room. That's where she spends most of her time these days."

I spot her immediately over by the window. She's staring through it in a trance, rocking back-and-forth in an over-sized lounge chair. An aide is bent over her, talking to her. I walk slowly across the room, my feet growing heavier with every step. Despite her incapacitated state, I can feel sweat prickling down my spine at the memory of being at her mercy in that isolated cabin.

"Hello, Brandy," I say, walking up to her.

She ignores me and continues to stare out the window.

The aide straightens up with an amused shake of her head. "I'll leave you two to talk. She has good days and bad days. Today's a bad day."

I flinch when Brandy adjusts the blanket in her lap and I catch sight of the reborn doll she's cradling. My chest heaves up and down, a deluge of sickening memories rushing back to mind.

Brandy smiles slyly up at me. "Isn't she beautiful?"

She throws a glance over her shoulder, then adds in a whisper. "Her name is Avery."

75

I can't stop shaking as I check into my hotel. I'm emotionally spent from dealing with Chad, who doesn't care enough to fight for his daughter, and my soon-to-be ex-sister-in-law who's obsessed with her. The doll creeps me out, but believing it's a real baby is a harmless delusion, given Brandy's incapacitated state. The part that nags at me—terrifies me—is that she named her doll Avery. How does she know my daughter's name? It couldn't be a coincidence, could it?

The nagging sensation in my gut tells me no. What else does she know about my daughter? And where is she getting this information from? I pace back-and-forth across my room for the best part of an hour before making the decision to drive home tonight. I can't be apart from my daughter a minute longer.

After tearing out of the hotel parking lot, I step on the gas, a feeling of panic spreading through my system like poisonous fumes. Laura is the only person who could have told her—which means she lied to me about cutting off all contact with Brandy. Fear blisters over my skin. Avery is alone with Laura. She knew I was going to visit Brandy today. She knew I would find out the truth—that she's been in contact with her daughter, and been feeding her information about Avery. What have I done? I've put my trust in the wrong person.

I hit the speed dial for Laura's number, but the phone rings and rings and goes straight to voicemail. I try Robin's number next, but she doesn't answer either. I'm in full panic mode now. I can tell by the horns beeping at me that I'm driving like a maniac. It's only a matter of time before a cop spots my antics and pulls me over. In my flustered state, I take the wrong exit off the freeway and end up having to backtrack, adding another half hour to the trip home.

I try to regulate my breathing, but my breath is coming in short hard gasps as though the oxygen is literally being squeezed from my lungs. I'll drive through the night if I have to. I desperately need to get home to my daughter—to hold her in my arms and know that she's safe. I can't believe I was stupid enough to leave her car seat with Laura. I made it easy for her to take my child. No wonder she said she didn't want to go with me to visit Brandy. She's been waiting on this opportunity.

When I finally arrive home, I squeal into the driveway and park with one wheel on the front lawn. I burst through the front door, yelling at the top of my lungs. "Laura, are you here?" I tear through the empty house, listening to the sound of my voice echoing off the walls. No response from Laura. I dash into the garage only to confirm my worst fear —her Chevy Blazer is gone! My heart sinks to the bottom of my stomach, and I feel like I'm dying. I try rationalizing with myself. Could she have taken Avery to the park? No! I told her not to go anywhere unless it was an emergency.

A tiny cry wafts through the house. A smidgen of hope

electrifies my senses. I vault up the stairs and into the nursery, my heart leaping when I spot movement in the crib.

I lunge toward it, then drop to my knees, every last vestige of hope leaking from me as I stare into the mocking face of a reborn doll.

76

The minutes and hours that follow blur into a nightmare with gnashing teeth. I feel hot and cold all at once, and I can't stop shaking as I stumble over my words to the even-keeled Detective Steele who's sitting opposite me at the kitchen table taking notes. Robin hovers at my side rubbing my arm as though the vibration might somehow soothe my mangled soul. Why did I ever put my faith in anyone in the Turner family?

Detective Steele's phone rings and she excuses herself for a moment. When she returns to the room, I can tell by the look on her face that something awful has happened. My entire body locks in one giant spasm of fear.

"No! No! No!" I repeat, shaking my head in a vain attempt to erase the reality I'm facing. "Don't tell me my daughter's dead."

Detective Steele clears her throat. "I've just been informed that Brandy Turner has escaped from Silvercrest Meadows."

My heart shoots into my mouth as shock decimates through me. "What? How is that even possible?"

Detective Steele grimaces. "She overpowered a night shift employee and stole her credentials and uniform, then deactivated the cameras while she made her escape in the employee's vehicle."

"How could they have allowed that to happen?" I scream at the detective.

"It wasn't a high security institution. Brandy wasn't considered a threat due to the fact that she had devolved into a childlike state after her brain injury. But it's obvious they underestimated her. She must have been planning the details for some time. They suspect she managed to avoid taking her medication."

"What are they doing to find her?" Robin asks, one arm tightly wrapped around my shaking shoulders.

"The institution has deployed staff to look for her—it doesn't appear that she's been back to her house. We also checked the cabin where she held her mother hostage. There's no indication she's been there either, but there are other remote cabins in that area where she could be hiding out. We've issued a BOLO, and alerted our officers to the fact that she's a risk to herself and others."

"A *risk*? How about a deadly threat?" I spit out. "She fooled you all. She's extremely dangerous and highly intelligent. She kidnapped her mother and me, tried to kill her mother, and had plans to kill me after Avery was born. She just escaped from a psychiatric institution. And all you can tell me is that you're going to be on the lookout!"

"I understand your frus—," Detective Steele begins, but I cut her off with a wave of my hand as I jump to my feet. "Just do your job and find her, and find my child!"

I stomp out of the kitchen in the direction of the garage.

Robin jogs after me. "Eva! Where are you going?" she

cries. "You can't just take off. What if they need to speak with you?"

"I'm going to find my daughter. Are you coming?"

Robin sighs. "Let me grab my purse."

When she disappears back inside the house, I pull out my phone and call the prison. "Can I speak to the warden, please. It's an emergency." It seems like an eternity before he comes on the line.

"Warden Gomez speaking."

"This is Eva Turner. My husband, Chad Turner, is incarcerated awaiting trial. Our daughter has been kidnapped by his sister. I need to speak with him. I need to know if he has any idea where she might have gone."

"I'm afraid without—"

"This is an emergency! The police are in my house. Do you want to speak to the detective in charge? Because I can put her on the phone right now!"

After a moment of silence, the warden says, "Give me a few minutes. Is this a good number for him to call you back on?"

"Yes, thank you. Thank you so much."

As I hang up, Robin slides into the passenger seat. "I told Detective Steele you needed some fresh air to clear your head. I don't think she would have appreciated knowing you were going to hunt for Brandy. The police are going to finish processing the house."

I start up the engine and back out of the garage. "I called the prison. The warden's going to have Chad call me back."

Robin turns to me, a look of consternation on her face. "What did you do that for? I thought you never wanted to speak to him again."

"I was desperate. He might have an idea where Brandy is. He hides a lot of of her secrets."

77

"I'm surprised to hear from you," Chad says. "Glad, but surprised.

I try not to burst into tears at the unexpected emotion that wells up inside me at the sound of his voice. " Brandy has escaped," I say. "She's taken our daughter—your mom too, I suspect."

There's a long silence on the other end of the line before Chad says, "You're not really giving our daughter up for adoption, are you?"

"No."

"I shouldn't be in here," Chad says in a strangled tone. "I should be out there helping you find her."

"Maybe you can still help. Can you think of anywhere Brandy might have gone? The police already checked the cabin and her house. Where else would she go to hide out. Maybe someplace from your childhood?"

"I can't think of anywhere in particular. Although, there was this old abandoned mining town we used to party at as teenagers—San Colima—until they boarded the place up. Brandy was fascinated by it. She'd always make weird comments, like it would be a great spot to hide a body. She said she would buy the town and live there if she ever won the lottery."

"Where is it?"

"About an hour and a half north, off the I-5."

"Got that?" I ask, turning to Robin who's busy punching it into the GPS.

She nods. "An hour and thirty-five minutes drive time from here."

I hang up after promising to let Chad know of any developments.

"Want me to grab some waters and snacks from the kitchen?" Robin asks.

"No. That'll only make Detective Steele suspicious. It's better if she thinks we're just going to drive around for a bit."

I back out of the garage and crawl past the squad cars parked at the curb. By the time we get on the I-5 and into the flow of traffic, the drive time has increased to an hour and forty-five minutes, and my heart rate is increasing at the same pace.

It's already dusk by the time we reach San Colima. The entry gate is padlocked and there's no sign of Brandy's car anywhere—just a few cows grazing nearby.

"Looks like this might have been a wasted trip," I say, resting my head on the steering wheel. I'm shattered and emotionally spent. I've lost everything, including the will to go on.

Robin gets out of the car and walks over to the wooden gate. She leans over it, wrestling with something and, a moment later, pushes it wide open.

"Someone cut the padlock off," she says, eyes gleaming as she clambers back into the car. "Brandy might be here after all."

I drive slowly through the gate, keeping my eyes peeled for any sign of Brandy's car, before coming to a stop next to an old wooden stagecoach parked in front of a dilapidated building. Robin and I exit the car and glance up and down the deserted street in both directions.

"Let's stick together," I say. "It's safer that way."

We fall silent as we start walking. At the end of the street, Robin spots an old outhouse at the back of a boarded-up storefront. "I'm going to check out the facilities," she says. She walks off in the direction of the outhouse, then suddenly turns around and darts back to me. "I see her car," she hisses, jabbing her finger dramatically behind the building.

"Let's check inside," I whisper.

"The front door's nailed shut. She must have gone in the back, or through a window," Robin says.

We tiptoe quietly around the side of the house to the back door. A rusted up broken bolt is lying in the dirt. I gingerly lift the wooden door and push it open, wincing at the scraping sound it makes. It's dark inside, but I'm reluctant to turn on my phone flashlight. It appears we're in a tumbledown store. The walls are lined with shelves of old tin cans, and dusty barrels are littered throughout. I pad across the floor, almost jumping out of my skin at a dark shape that turns out to be a dress form.

Robin comes up behind me, eyes wide in her pale face. "Where could they be?"

We both freeze at the sound of an infant's cry.

I put a finger to my lips and point to a rickety staircase at the far end of the store.

I lead the way up the uneven stairs, coming to a sudden halt at the sight that greets me. Laura is sitting on the floor with her hands tied in front of her. There's an ugly matted clot on the side of her head that looks suspiciously like blood. Avery is in her car seat next to her, squirming and mewling softly.

My psycho sister-in-law stands guard in front of them, feet braced, and brandishing a knife.

78

I raise my hands in an attitude of surrender. "Brandy, let's all stay calm and we can talk this through."

"How did you find me?" she seethes. "How could you possibly have known I was here? It was my little brother, wasn't it? I should have killed that snake when I had the chance."

"He doesn't want to hurt you. He wants to fix the situation and get you the help you need. We all do."

"Are *you* here to help me?" Brandy sneers. "I doubt it."

I wet my lips, rooting around for something soothing to say. She still hasn't lowered the knife.

"I know the kind of help you're offering," Brandy goes on. "You've got the police out there, haven't you?"

"No. I left the cops behind at my house. They thought I went out for a drive to clear my head. It's just us, Brandy. Put down the knife and let's talk."

Her eyes dart from me to Robin. "Why's she here?"

"I want to help too," Robin interjects. "We're in this together—all three of us. You and I planned Eva's bridal shower, remember? We can work this out."

"And what exactly would that look like, Robin? Would you like to drag me back to my psychiatric prison and drug me until I'm so zombiefied I don't even remember my name? Because that's what they do to people in there. They medicate away your humanity."

"I'm not a doctor, I'm just your friend," Robin says. "I'd like you to put down the knife for starters, so we can sit down and talk about this."

Avery whimpers, arching her back as she sticks her tiny fists into the air. I can tell she's getting ready to launch into a full-blown crying bout.

"Avery's upset," I say. "She might be hungry, or need changing. Can you please let me pick her up so I can try to comfort her at least?"

Brandy's face contorts into a malevolent expression. "Are you saying I don't know how to look after my baby?"

I fight to keep my tone neutral. This isn't the moment to argue over ownership of Avery. "This is no place to bring a baby," I say, glancing around the room. "Where's her diaper bag?"

Brandy wets her lips. "Laura forgot it. She's a useless grandmother. You really shouldn't leave your child with her. She doesn't know what she's doing."

Laura looks at me with red-rimmed eyes. Her shoulders shake as she weeps silently.

"Can I please pick Avery up?" I ask. "It's hard to hear each other above her cries."

"No! Don't touch her!" Brandy says, pointing the knife at me. "She's mine!"

"You're never going to get away with this," I say. "You can't just take someone's child. I'm her biological mother. No court in the land would rule in your favor."

Brandy twists her lips, a look of grim determination

settling over her face. "If I can't have her, neither will you." She spins around and raises the knife over the car seat.

I let out a guttural scream, watching the scene unfold in slow motion as Laura throws herself protectively over the car seat. The knife comes down hard in her back.

Adrenaline floods my system and, before I know what's happening, I'm body slamming Brandy to the ground.

79

Three months later

"Happy birth-day, dear Laura! Happy birthday to you!"

I hoot and holler, and clap and cheer, along with Robin and several of Laura's friends—this time in all sincerity. I'm thankful to be hosting my mother-in-law's birthday and not her funeral.

Avery claps her hands in her highchair, gurgling in delight at all the commotion. At six months old, she's the happiest and most beautiful child I could ever have wished for. And I have Laura to thank that she's still here with us. She saved my daughter's life at the risk of losing her own. Thankfully, the knife Brandy plunged into her missed her vital organs, but she almost bled to death before the emergency services reached her.

"Any word on Chad's release?" Robin asks as I'm refilling the punch bowl.

"His lawyer says it will be any day now," I say.

In light of Brandy's unreliability as a witness, Chad's case was dismissed. It was her word against his. Other than her testimony, there was no convincing evidence to convict him of foul play in Shana's death. But it doesn't give me any reassurance that he wasn't involved.

"How do you feel about Chad getting out?" Robin asks.

"I'm reserving judgement. We'll just have to see how it goes."

"He can hardly kill you now for the life insurance—it would look pretty obvious," Robin says, quirking a grin.

I grimace. "That's so not funny. Anyway, we canceled the policies. It was a mutual agreement."

"So, are you going to let him see Avery?"

"Court-ordered supervised visits only. I'm going to be the most obnoxious hypervigilant mother ever. Avery's never getting out of my sight again."

"Not even to hang out with her Aunt Robin?" my sister asks, with a twinkle in her eye.

I chuckle. "It might be up for negotiation—at some point. I'm not ready yet."

"You don't have to worry anymore," Robin says. "Brandy's never getting out of the high security psychiatric facility she's in this time, at least not alive. She'll never get near Avery again."

"I can't count on that one-hundred-percent. She's brilliant—she managed to find out Avery's name before she kidnapped her. She called Rose at work to get the correct spelling, pretending she was from a flower and balloon company. I thought Laura must have given her the name, but I should have known Brandy would be way more devious than that. I feel bad now for thinking the worst of Laura, but I'll never forget the sense of panic that gripped me when I thought she'd taken Avery."

"I told you not to marry into that family," Robin says. " There were too many red flags from the beginning."

I give a thoughtful nod. "And too many secrets. I've learned my lesson. I'll never trust anyone other than you again."

"You can't close people out forever. You might miss out on the love of your life."

I let out a heavy sigh. "I thought that's what I had with Chad."

"Maybe you can rebuild it."

I shake my head. "Sometimes things are irrevocably damaged. Even if I give him the benefit of the doubt, I'll never fully trust him again. He destroyed my trust in other people, too."

"You're going to make life hard for Avery if you don't move beyond that," Robin says.

"How can I trust anyone when I don't even trust my own judgment? I married Chad against everyone's advice, and look what happened. I wish someone would invent a trust thermometer so you could just take everyone's temperature and know what you're getting into."

Robin laughs. "All I can tell you is to keep on trying. Sometimes relationships break, and the pieces may never look the same, but you can try and make something new out of them."

The doorbell rings and I go to answer it. Shock decimates through me when I see who's standing on the steps. Chad holds up a couple of gifts, a goofy grin on his face. "I brought something for Mom, and this one was on the doorstep." He clears his throat. "I'd love to see our daughter, just for a minute or two."

"You can't come in. I don't want you to meet her yet. It isn't the right time."

His smile falters but he gives an acquiescent nod. "I

understand." He passes me the gifts. "Give my baby girl a hug from me."

I walk back into the house, dragging my feet behind me. I don't know if it was the right thing to do to turn him away, but it didn't feel like the right thing to invite him in either. He's fresh out of prison, and I can't rule out the possibility that he might have killed his first wife.

"That was Chad," I say as I walk back into the room clutching the gifts. "He wanted to meet Avery, but he didn't push it when I told him it was too soon."

Robin gives an approving nod. "You did the right thing."

I set the gifts on the table next to the other ones.

Robin peeks at the tags. "This one's for Avery," she says, handing it back to me. "It doesn't say who it's from."

Frowning, I sink down in a chair and rip open the pink polka dot wrapping paper on the gift to reveal a white box. I carefully remove the lid and pull out the tissue paper.

A chill shoots up my spine when the unblinking eyes of a reborn doll stare up at me.

A QUICK FAVOR

Dear Reader,

I hope you enjoyed reading *The Bridal Shower* as much as I enjoyed writing it. Thank you for taking the time to check out my books and I would appreciate it from the bottom of my heart if you would leave a review on Amazon or Goodreads as it makes a HUGE difference in helping new readers find the series. Thank you!

To be the first to hear about my upcoming book releases, sales, and fun giveaways, join my newsletter at **https://normahinkens.-com/newsletter**

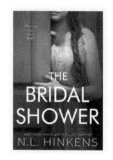

and follow me on Twitter, Instagram and Facebook. Feel free to email me at norma@normahinkens.com with any feedback or comments. I LOVE hearing from readers. YOU are the reason I keep writing!

All my best,

Norma

THE PICKLEBALL KILLER

Check out *The Pickleball Killer, the first book in the **Cunning Crimes Collection***! Releasing April 2026.

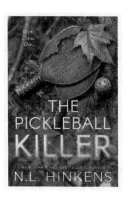

The court is a dangerous place ...

Dr. Amber Cunningham is a well-respected psychologist with a seemingly perfect life and a passion for pickleball. But when her best friend, Maya, is discovered dead on the grounds of the Bayfront Pickleball Club, her world quickly begins to unravel.

Suspicion falls on a controversial new member who recently joined the club. She's not who she says she is—but then neither is Amber. She's managed to keep her darkest secrets under wraps until now, but long buried rivalry and resentment simmer beneath the surface.

The closer Amber gets to the truth of Maya's death, the more dangerous things become for her. In desperation she confides in the other women at the club. The problem with secrets is that someone always spills them.

Now she faces the terrifying possibility that the killer is one of them.

- A compulsive thriller that will leave your heart pounding and your jaw on the floor! -

Will you enjoy The Pickleball Killer? If you read any of my favorite psychological and domestic suspense thriller authors including K.L. Slater, Shalini Boland, Kiersten Modglin, Freida McFadden, Kathryn Croft, Lisa Gardner, Louise Jensen, Gregg Olsen, Mark Edwards, or Rachel Caine, the answer is a resounding yes!

WHAT TO READ NEXT

Ready for another thrilling read with shocking twists and a mind-blowing murder plot?

Explore my entire lineup of thrillers on Amazon or at
https://normahinkens.com/thrillers

Do you enjoy reading across genres? I also write young adult science fiction and fantasy thrillers. You can find out more about those titles at
https://normahinkens.com/YAbooks

BIOGRAPHY

NYT and USA Today bestselling author N. L. Hinkens writes twisty psychological suspense thrillers with unexpected endings. She's a travel junkie, coffee hound, and idea wrangler, in no particular order. She grew up in Ireland—land of legends and storytelling—and now resides in the US. Her work has won the Grand Prize Next Generation Indie Book Award for fiction, as well as numerous other awards. Check out her newsletter for hot new releases, stellar giveaways, exclusive content, behind the scenes and more.

https://normahinkens.com/newsletter

Follow her on Facebook for funnies, giveaways, cool stuff & more!

https://normahinkens.com/Facebook

BOOKS BY N. L. HINKENS

SHOP THE ENTIRE CATALOG HERE

https://normahinkens.com/thrillers

VILLAINOUS VACATIONS COLLECTION

- The Cabin Below
- You Will Never Leave
- Her Last Steps

DOMESTIC DECEPTIONS COLLECTION

- Never Tell Them
- I Know What You Did
- The Other Woman

PAYBACK PASTS COLLECTION

- The Class Reunion
- The Lies She Told
- Right Behind You

TREACHEROUS TRIPS COLLECTION

- Wrong Exit
- The Invitation
- While She Slept

WICKED WAYS COLLECTION

- All But Safe
- What You Wish For

- The Bridal Shower

<u>CUNNING CRIMES COLLECTION</u>

- The Pickleball Killer

<u>NOVELLAS</u>

- The Silent Surrogate

BOOKS BY NORMA HINKENS

I also write young adult science fiction and fantasy thrillers under Norma Hinkens.

https://normahinkens.com/YAbooks

THE UNDERGROUNDERS SERIES
POST-APOCALYPTIC

- Immurement
- Embattlement
- Judgement

THE EXPULSION PROJECT
SCIENCE FICTION

- Girl of Fire
- Girl of Stone
- Girl of Blood

Books by Norma Hinkens

THE KEEPERS CHRONICLES
EPIC FANTASY

- Opal of Light
- Onyx of Darkness
- Opus of Doom

FOLLOW NORMA

FOLLOW NORMA:

Sign up for her newsletter:
https://normahinkens.com/newsletter
Website:
https://normahinkens.com/
Facebook:
https://normahinkens.com/Facebook
Twitter
https://normahinkens.com/Twitter
Instagram
https://normahinkens.com/Instagram
Pinterest:
https://normahinkens.com/Pinterest

Made in the USA
Columbia, SC
18 May 2025